GAINING MILES

A MILES FAMILY NOVELLA

CLAIRE KINGSLEY

ISBN: 9781095292198

Published by Always Have, LLC

Edited by Elayne Morgan of Serenity Editing Services

Cover Image by Kari March

www.clairekingsleybooks.com

 Created with Vellum

For all my readers who loved Ben and Shannon from the start. This is for you.

ABOUT THIS BOOK

"Now there was nothing holding me back. I kissed her deeply, passionately. Kissed her for every time I'd wanted to and couldn't. For every time I'd stared at her with longing in my heart, wishing we could be where we were now."

It's never too late.

Loving a woman you can't have isn't easy. I endured the slow torture of watching Shannon Miles live a life with another man —a man who didn't deserve her—but I don't regret a minute of it. And I have my reasons.

Now, she's free. No longer shackled to a loveless marriage, bound to someone who was unfaithful and heartless.

But Shannon thinks her time has passed. That she won't get another chance at love, especially not with the man who's been there to see it all. The hurt. The mistakes. The heartache.

If only she knew. I love that woman with everything I am, and I want nothing more in this life than to spend every moment with her.

It's time for our happily ever after.

ONE

BEN

TWENTY-SIX YEARS ago

THE SOUND of a giggling toddler was unexpected this deep in the vineyard. I'd come out here to walk among the vines. Find some solitude in the fragrant late-summer air. The other workers had gone in, and I hadn't seen a soul. So why did I suddenly hear a baby's laugh?

The owners had kids, but I'd never seen them up close. Kept my distance from the family, although they lived here, on this beautiful piece of property. But getting to know people wasn't why I was here. I was here to disappear.

That, and make a little money. A man needed to eat, after all. And a job working at a winery in a tiny town in the mountains was as good a job as any. Better than most, really. Not many questions. Hard work, but I wasn't afraid of that. And space. Lots of space. Perfect for days like today when the weight on my shoulders felt like it might crush me.

Walking helped.

There was that baby giggle again. I stopped and a bee buzzed past my ear. Had I imagined it? Was I further gone than I'd thought? It had sounded like a little boy.

"Mama?"

There was no quaver in that little voice. No indication he was scared. I walked up the row of vines, in the direction of the sound. Leaves rustled. Then a bump.

Rounding a corner, I saw the source of the noise. A little boy, naked as the day he was born, sitting in the dirt. He had wispy light brown hair, pudgy cheeks, and a round belly. He looked up at me with enormous blue eyes—eyes that seemed to hold the entire sky—and smiled. Dimples puckered his cheeks, and he laughed.

"I dirty," he said, holding out his hands for me to see. They were indeed covered with dirt.

"You sure are. What are you doing out here by yourself, little man?"

He didn't answer, just kept grinning at me.

"Where's your mommy?" I asked.

"I dunno." He gave me a dramatic shrug, dirty palms up, his blue eyes big and wide.

He must have been one of the Miles kids. They had a few. Three boys, if I recalled. This one was probably about two years old.

I glanced around, my ears straining for the sound of footsteps. His mother had to be close by. We were a long way from the main grounds and the house where the Miles family lived. How did this little guy get out here?

"Bye-bye!"

My head whipped around just in time to see the naked little boy disappearing between the vines.

"Oh shit."

I darted after him. He wasn't my kid—and seeing him dug at wounds I'd have much rather left buried—but I couldn't just leave him. I couldn't get through the gap, so I ran up ahead and doubled back. He wasn't far ahead, but those chubby little legs moved fast. He cast a glance back at me, squealed at the top of his lungs, and ran faster.

"You little stinker."

A few long strides and I was on him. I scooped him up, ignoring his flailing arms and kicking legs. He laughed hysterically, like we were playing the best game.

His laugh was infectious. How long had it been since I'd laughed? I couldn't remember. It rumbled deep in my chest, as if it was clearing cobwebs out of my soul.

"All right kid. Let's go find your mama."

"Mama?"

"Yeah, little man. Where is she?"

"Home," he said happily.

I highly doubted she was all the way back at the family home. But I didn't see any sign of her as I headed toward the main grounds. The little boy stopped struggling, so I adjusted him, holding him upright on my hip. It occurred to me that I had no idea if the kid was potty trained.

"Don't pee on me, okay, little man?"

"Outside," he said. "I go pee outside."

He sounded so proud of himself, I couldn't help but laugh again. "Good for you. I suppose that's as good a place as any."

Finally, the vineyard opened to the main grounds. A few vineyard workers were heading back toward the cellars, but no sign of the kid's parents. Taking him home was probably my best option. I just hoped his mom wasn't out in the vineyard behind me, looking for him.

"Cooper?" A woman's voice rang out from somewhere to

my left, a note of panic in her tone. "Cooper? Baby boy, where'd you go? Cooper?"

"Are you Cooper?" I asked.

He nodded. "Mama?"

"Yeah, let's go see Mama."

I hurried in the direction of her voice. She called out again, the fear in her tone spurring me to move faster.

"Ma'am," I called out. "Ma'am, I think I have your son."

She burst out from a trail, sweat gleaming on her forehead, her eyes wide with worry. "Oh my god, Cooper."

He reached for her, practically diving out of my arms. She caught him, like the expert toddler-wrangler she obviously was.

"Cooper, you can't run away like that. You have to stay with Mommy." She held him close, pressing one hand to his back.

"I dirty," he said, looking proud as ever of his dirty hands.

"I see that. Where are your clothes?"

"I don't know. I like naked."

She let out a heavy sigh, her eyes darting up, like she was asking the Lord for strength. "I know you like being naked. But baby boy, you need to leave your clothes on. More importantly, you need to stay with Mommy. I was scared to death."

"He got me," Cooper said, pointing straight at me.

His mother looked at me, her features softening. She was beautiful, with long dark hair and clear blue eyes. My heart squeezed at the sight of her, my chest aching with a feeling I hadn't experienced in a long time. I hadn't been sure there was still a heart in there. It reminded me of its existence now, thumping so hard it made the blood roar in my ears.

"Thank you," she said. "Thank you so much. I'm so sorry, Cooper's a handful. I only turned my back for a second."

"It's no trouble. I saw him out there and figured a naked two-year-old probably belonged to someone nearby."

She nodded, adjusting Cooper on her hip. "I'm Shannon. Shannon Miles. Obviously you've met my son, Cooper."

I dipped my chin. Would have tipped my hat, had I been wearing one. "Benjamin Gaines." I went by Ben. Wasn't sure why I'd given her my full name like that.

"It's nice to meet you, Benjamin. Would you like to come over to the house? I made cookies."

"Cookies?" Cooper asked, his face lighting up with so much joy, it was hard not to agree—cookies sounded like the best thing in the world when he said it like that.

But making friends with these people wasn't a good idea. I wouldn't be here long. A season, maybe two, then I'd move on. I always had to move on. It was the only way.

"No, that's—"

"Cookies," Cooper said, looking me straight in the eyes. His little voice was suddenly so serious, a baffling depth of meaning hidden in that one little word. It was as if he'd said, *You need to come have cookies with me, Ben, your life depends on it.*

I stared at the little boy in his mother's arms. His bright blue eyes watched me as if my answer to this request meant the world to him. For reasons I couldn't possibly fathom, I didn't want to let him down.

"Sure," I said, pulling my gaze away from his hypnotic eyes. "I'd love a cookie."

"Cookie," Cooper said, his tone assured, as if that settled the matter.

I followed them down the low hill, the back of their house coming into view. It was a beautiful home—from the outside, anyway—with a big wrap-around porch and a garden in the back. Shannon's two other boys were there, playing near the raised beds. Or the younger one was playing, at least. Her oldest son watched his mother with crossed arms, his brow furrowed. He looked so serious for a child who could only be around six.

"Where was Cooper?" he asked.

"In the vineyard," Shannon said. "This is Benjamin. He found him."

The boy marched toward me and stuck out his arm. It took me a second to realize what he wanted. I clasped his hand and shook.

"I'm Roland Miles," he said. "That's my brother Leo."

"You have very proper manners, Roland Miles," I said. "I'm Ben."

The other little boy, Leo, had lighter hair—almost blond—but the same blue eyes. He sat in the dirt surrounded by little toy cars. He drove two into each other, making crashing noises and spitting. His eyes darted up to mine and he smiled, but didn't seem interested in a handshake greeting like his brother.

Shannon put Cooper down, grabbed a pair of shorts that were sitting nearby, and pulled them on him. "You stay put, you hear me? Or no cookie."

"Okay, Mommy."

She glanced at Roland. "I'm going inside to get cookies and lemonade. Can you watch your brother for two minutes?"

"Yes," Roland said. Shannon jogged around the side of the house, and Roland rolled his eyes. "Cooper won't keep his clothes on. And he runs away every time."

"Sounds like your baby brother is a handful."

Roland sighed. "You have no idea."

The little one didn't seem like he was a flight risk now. Maybe the promise of a cookie was enough to keep him still.

I sat down on the edge of a raised garden bed. I probably shouldn't have stayed. It felt odd to sit out here with these kids. Hurt in places I didn't want to feel. I'd have to take a cookie to be polite, then be on my way. Keep my distance from now on.

Cooper wandered over to me, and as if he'd known me his

whole life, crawled right up into my lap. He patted my beard with his little hand and smiled. "Hi, Ben."

In that moment, Cooper Miles broke me.

The hard shell I'd constructed around my heart cracked wide open. It was as if a rush of fresh air surged through me, cleaning out the cold, empty spaces I'd closed off. For years, I'd kept that armor around my heart, sure it was the only way I'd survive. Stay alone. Don't let anyone inside.

That little boy made me crumble with just a pat to my chin.

I swallowed hard, overcome with a sudden rush of emotion. Cooper rubbed his palm against my facial hair, giggling, like it tickled. His laugh was so light, his smile so pure.

I'd met their father, Lawrence. He'd hired me. It was hard to believe this joyful little spark had come from that man. From what I knew of Lawrence Miles, he was serious and demanding. I'd worked for worse, but the idea of this bright little boy being raised by a man like him made my chest ache.

For reasons I didn't understand, I desperately wanted Cooper to keep whatever it was that burned so brightly inside him.

Roland glanced at me again and his little shoulders relaxed. He sat down next to Leo and grabbed a car. It was as if he'd let his guard down and could finally play. Was it because I had his brother? It was hard to be sure.

Leo crashed his car into Roland's and the two erupted with laughter. Cooper kicked his legs and laughed along with his brothers.

Shannon came around the side of the house carrying a tray with a plate of cookies, a pitcher of lemonade, and a stack of plastic cups. "Okay, here we are."

"Cookies!" Cooper exclaimed.

She set the tray on the edge of another garden bed. Roland and Leo sprang up and stood in front of her.

"Your hands are filthy, but... oh well." She handed them each a cookie and a cup of lemonade, then looked over at Cooper, still sitting in my lap. "Wow. He must like you. He doesn't do that very often."

"Doesn't do what?"

"Sit. He's either moving or sleeping. There's not much in between." She grabbed two cookies and brought them over, handing one to Cooper, the other to me. "Thank you again. I know a cookie isn't really enough thanks, but it's the best I can do on short notice."

I adjusted Cooper in my lap. The weight of his little body was comforting, somehow. As were the satisfied smiles of the other boys. "No need for anything else. This is perfect."

By the time I finished my cookie, Cooper's brief adventure in sitting still was over. He scrambled down from my lap, darted for the tray, snatched another cookie, and tried to run.

But I was faster than he was. I caught him around the waist and spun him around while he squealed with delight.

"Nice try, little man."

"Oh, Cooper," Shannon said. The poor woman sounded so tired. "Okay, buddy. Containment strategy number two. Time to go inside."

I helped her bring the snack into the house. It felt awkward to be in her home, so I quickly made for the door. Stopping in the doorway, I nodded to her.

"Thanks again for the snack. I'll see you around."

"Thank you so much, Benjamin," she said amid the chaos erupting at her feet. Cooper clung to one leg and Leo tugged on her shirt, trying to ask her a question. "Leo, wait one minute, please. Cooper, can you let go of my leg, honey? Mommy needs to walk."

I shut the door with a soft click and made my way down the porch steps.

Shannon Miles didn't know it, but her little boys had done something to me. Reminded me that a heart still beat in my chest. That maybe my life hadn't ended.

I let out a long breath as I walked to my truck. The sun was sinking toward the mountain peaks that surrounded Salishan Cellars, the air already cooling. And something told me that wasn't the last time I'd chase down a naked Cooper Miles in the vineyard.

TWO

BEN

PRESENT DAY

SPARKS DANCED into the night sky, carried up by currents of air I couldn't feel. The fire blazed hot, licking the edges of my mattress, the coals at the bottom glowing bright red. I'd stacked wood around the base to keep it going even once the mattress itself burned out. Made for a nice big bonfire.

I sat back in my chair, one foot crossed over my knee, bottle of beer in my hand. I had a feeling my solitude wouldn't last. One of the boys was bound to catch a whiff of the fire, or see the sparks rise, their orange and red lights winking in the darkness. I'd brought a six-pack, expecting company.

Then again, any or all of them might be otherwise occupied tonight. It wasn't like there was a horde of bachelors roaming Salishan's acres these days. One by one, all my kids had found love and settled down.

Of course, technically they weren't *my* kids. I hadn't fathered them. And I'd never spoken of them that way out loud.

But I'd stopped beating myself up for thinking of them as mine years ago. I wasn't their father, but they were mine just the same. I'd been a part of their lives—watching out for them— since they were little. Since that day, so many years ago, when I'd chased a naked two-year-old Cooper through the vineyard and brought him back to his mother.

Shannon.

Her name drifted through my mind like a cool breeze. Soothing. Beautiful. Shannon Miles, the woman I'd loved from afar for longer than was strictly healthy.

She'd been through hell the last couple of years. As happy as I'd been to see her husband go, I'd hated the pain it had brought her. He'd been unfaithful off and on throughout most of their marriage. I hadn't known. Oh, I'd suspected. Strongly. But I'd told myself over and over that it was none of my business. I had no place getting in between a married man and woman.

That was one of my life's biggest regrets. If I'd trusted my gut and exposed Lawrence years ago, maybe I could have saved her, and those kids, a hell of a lot of pain.

But then again, it was hard to say how that would have turned out. Maybe she wouldn't have believed me. Maybe she wouldn't have been ready to hear the truth. Maybe the crushing responsibility of being a single mother to four young kids while trying to keep her family's winery afloat would have made her even more miserable than her husband had.

I doubted it, but it gave me some comfort to think I hadn't ruined her life by keeping out of it.

Shannon had been the name my heart had whispered for a long time. I hadn't always loved her. The first time we spoke, that day on the edge of the vineyard when Cooper had run off, hadn't been the moment I'd fallen for her. I'd noticed her, and maybe deep down, a part of me had known I'd love her one day.

But back then, she was a married young mother, as unavailable as a person could get.

No, I fell for her kids first. They were the reason I'd stayed. Back in those days, I'd been little more than a drifter. No permanent home, no ties to anything. I'd wanted it that way, thinking I could outrun the pain of my past. The Miles kids had given me a reason to plant roots. I'd stayed here for them, and I'd never regretted it.

However, watching Shannon live a life with another man—especially a piece of shit like Lawrence Miles—had been a special kind of torture.

But now, Lawrence was gone. It had been a long, hard road for Shannon. His selfishness had come back to haunt not only her, but her entire family. Fortunately, justice had prevailed, and their ordeal was over.

And today, I'd decided it was time.

I heard the boys—Cooper and Chase, if I wasn't mistaken—coming down the path to the clearing. Probably giving each other shit, by their tones and the laughter that followed. Chase was one of mine in much the same way the Miles kids always had been. He and Cooper had been best friends since they were five. In our own ways—separately, of course—Shannon and I had adopted Chase as one of ours. Now that he was married to Brynn, he was a Miles in everything but name. Although really, he always had been.

"Ben, dude, what's going on out here?" Cooper asked, dragging a chair over. He didn't sit down. "Having a party without us? What's up with that? I know we've been busy or whatever, but still. Have some manners, man. Give a guy a heads up."

"Coop." Chase tried to get Cooper's attention.

"I guess the beer makes up for it, though. Beer me, good buddy."

I opened a beer and handed it to Cooper. Chase looked at the fire, then at me, then back at the fire.

"Um, Coop?"

Cooper dropped into the chair and took a long swig. "I can't stay too long. Cookie's at the ranch late tonight. She's been there all day, and I miss the fuck out of her. So fair warning, as soon as she texts me that she's on her way home, I'm bailing on you guys. Sorry if that violates bro code."

"Cooper," Chase said, his voice sharp.

"What? Get a chair and grab a beer, bro. What's wrong with you?"

"Look." He pointed at the fire.

Cooper's head swiveled toward the fire and his eyes widened. He looked at me, the flames dancing in his eyes. "Dude."

I waited. Cooper was about to unload a verbal assault and it was always better to let him do it, then speak afterward. But he stayed quiet.

Had I actually rendered Cooper Miles speechless?

A big smile crossed Chase's face. "Fuck yes. Fuck. Yes."

"Fuck yes, indeed, boys," I said and took a drink.

"Took you long enough," Cooper said.

"Don't start with me, Coop," I said.

He put up his hands, as if in surrender. "I know, I know. Your clocks need to be in sync. I get it. You were right about me and Amelia. But what changed?"

I took another drink, pondering my answer. "Well, her divorce is final, although it's more than that. Things were hard for a while, but they've settled down. And like you said, our clocks need to be in sync."

"And they are now?" Cooper asked.

"I hope so. And if they aren't, maybe I'm ready to give hers a nudge in the right direction."

Cooper grinned at me. "This is awesome. Do you know how awesome this is? There are definitely parts of this that I don't need to know, or talk about, because it's my mom. But I'm really fucking happy for you."

"Don't get ahead of yourself," I said. "I'm not out here burning this thing because I put a ring on her finger."

"Holy shit, Ben," Chase said. "Are you going to propose?"

"You know what this means, right?" Cooper asked, the firelight reflecting in his wide eyes. "If you marry my mom, you'll be my stepdad."

"And my father-in-law," Chase said.

"Slow down, boys. I haven't even asked her out on a date yet. All this," I said, gesturing to the fire, "is just symbolic."

"Yeah, we get it," Chase said. "But I still think you should marry her."

"Chase, I love how pro-marriage you are," Cooper said. "And I agree, he should definitely marry my mom."

"Hell yes, I'm pro-marriage," Chase said. "Speaking of, what gives? Are you going to lock shit down with Amelia or what?"

Cooper crossed an ankle over his knee. "Our love is solid. I don't need to lock it down to know she's mine forever. Don't get me wrong, I'm marrying the shit out of that girl—when she's ready."

Chase nodded. "I can respect that."

"So where are you taking her?" Cooper asked, looking at me. "On your first date, I mean. You better make it good, dude. This is a long time coming, and my mom hasn't been on a date in a long-ass time."

"I thought I'd take her to dinner, but now you're making me wonder if that's good enough."

"Dinner's good," Cooper said. "But be sure she knows it's a date, not a friend thing."

"Yeah, you've been in the friend-zone forever," Chase said. "It could be tough to climb out."

"That's a good point," Cooper said. "I'm glad we noticed you out here tonight because you're definitely going to need our help."

"Cooper Miles, I do not need dating help from you," I said, although Chase's friend-zone comment had gotten under my skin a little.

"Why not?" Cooper asked. "I'm awesome at this stuff."

I raised an eyebrow and took a drink.

"You are awesome at it, Coop, but I gotta be honest," Chase said. "I think Ben has this covered. Look at him."

Cooper eyed me for a few seconds. "He *is* handsome as hell. He's been rocking the beard since before beards were cool. And the gray just makes him look distinguished."

"Exactly," Chase said. "The dude's a panty-melter even without our help."

"I agree with you, but can we not talk about panties when the panties being melted in this case belong to my mom?" Cooper asked.

"Good point," Chase said.

Shaking my head, I laughed. These two. I loved these boys. Life wouldn't have been the same without them. But I didn't need their advice when it came to dating.

This didn't need to be complicated. I was going to approach Shannon and ask her out on a date, like a man should. Take her out. Treat her right. There was still that bit of doubt in my mind —concern that maybe Chase was right. Maybe I was just a friend. And maybe that was all I'd ever be to her.

But what I felt for her was too big to ignore. Too much to contain. I'd watched Shannon from afar for so long. Now there was nothing keeping us apart. I was going to take the chance. Put my heart on the line. I'd give it to her if she wanted it. Give it all to her and never ask for it back. I wasn't sure if Cooper and Chase had been joking when they said I should marry her. But that was absolutely what I wanted. Only one question remained. Would she have me?

Soon, I'd find out.

THREE

SHANNON

HUDSON WAS fast asleep in my lap, soothed by the motion of the rocking chair. My arms were tired from holding him, but I wasn't about to get up. There was nothing like holding a sleeping baby, and I was positively smitten with this little guy. He was eight months old now, and threatening to crawl. Roland and Zoe's life was about to get a lot more interesting when he got mobile.

They'd gone out for a date night. I loved that they lived close for many reasons—seeing my grandson included. But even more than that, I loved that I could give them time together. Their commitment to each other—and their marriage—as they navigated the transition into parenthood was heartwarming to see.

I heard the front door open and close. A few seconds later, footsteps ascending the stairs. It sounded like Roland.

My son peeked through Hudson's half-open door and smiled. He was thirty-three years old with a wife and child, and I still looked at him and wondered how he'd gotten so tall. He favored his father—only much more handsome—with dark hair, blue eyes, and that neatly trimmed stubble so many men were wearing these days. It suited him.

As did fatherhood.

"Hey, Mom," he said, his voice soft. "Sorry to keep you here so long."

"It's fine." I glanced down at Hudson. His eyelashes brushed his round cheeks and his lips moved in his sleep. "He's been asleep for about an hour."

"Thanks." He gently lifted Hudson out of my lap and cradled him in his arms, swaying a little. "I'll get him down for the night."

I loved seeing Roland as a father. The love and care in his eyes when he gazed at his son filled my heart. I left him to it, quietly slipping out the door as he snuggled his baby boy.

Zoe was downstairs. She smiled and hugged me when I came into the kitchen. "Thanks again for watching him."

"Did you have a nice date?"

"We did," she said. "Dinner was delicious. And no one needed to be burped. It's so nice to feel like a woman, not just a mom. Even if it's only for a few hours."

"It's good for you."

"Thanks." She smiled again and gave me another hug.

With their baby asleep, I knew they probably wanted more privacy, so I said my goodbyes. Roland came downstairs just as I was leaving, so I got a hug from my son, too. I left them in their cozy house, their sweet baby asleep upstairs.

And it made me happy.

They lived a short drive from Salishan. All my kids were close, which was a dream come true. Now that my divorce was final, Chase and Brynn could start on the house they had planned—right on Salishan land. Cooper would do the same, although he and Amelia seemed happy to live in one of the guest cottages for the time being.

Leo and Hannah were still contemplating their living situation. With a baby on the way, eventually they'd need more space than they had now. Like I'd done for my other kids, I was going to offer them a parcel of the land to build on. I had a feeling they'd take me up on it.

I parked in front of my house and went inside. Took off my coat and put down my purse. I'd skipped dinner, so my first order of business for the evening was finding something to eat.

My kitchen was spacious, with cupboard doors worn from years of use, gray counter tops, and a small kitchen table next to the window. I still had my mother's collection of tea cups and more wine glasses than I knew what to do with.

I opened the fridge and was surprised to find a container of leftover chicken. For a woman who lived alone, my leftovers disappeared remarkably fast. But my boys still stopped by, sniffing around the kitchen for lunch or a snack. They knew I cooked more than I needed and was happy to share.

The truth was, I did it on purpose. I cooked so much because I liked giving them an excuse to come over. Cooper and Chase were regulars in my kitchen, even now that neither of them was a bachelor. Leo too. Before Hannah, I'd often tried to tempt him out of hiding with the promise of leftovers or a big batch of homemade muffins. Now that he had Hannah in his life, I didn't feel like it was necessary to try to coax him out of his house.

But I still cooked a lot.

I warmed up the chicken, poured a glass of wine, and took it to my kitchen table. I preferred eating in here when I was alone. My dining table was big—it could easily seat twelve, more if we squished—and when I sat there by myself it felt immense. And very empty.

A quiet house was a nice change after an evening watching my grandson. I loved spending time with him, but my days raising little boys were long over. Being a grandma was perfect—I got lots of baby snuggles, without the hard work that went into parenting. Even on days when I watched him, I got to come home to my regular life. A life where my children were adults.

Not just adults—settled adults. Roland, once again married to Zoe, raising their first child. My baby girl, Brynn, married to Chase—who'd been like a son to me since he was five. Leo and Hannah would be getting married soon, and my second grandchild was on the way. And Cooper. That whirlwind of chaos and energy that was my youngest son had actually met his match in Amelia.

All four of my children were in love and happy. And after the example they'd grown up with, that seemed like a miracle.

Thirty-five years ago, when I'd married Lawrence Miles, I couldn't have imagined my life would turn out the way it had. I'd been young and hopeful, swept off my feet by a man with ambition. In Lawrence, I'd seen stability. Someone who would support my passion for my family's business and provide for the family I'd always known I wanted.

What I'd gotten was a man who'd quickly become cold and distant, not long after our wedding. Who'd been unfaithful to me. Fathered children with another woman and kept that family a secret from all of us. Who'd almost run my family's winery into the ground with his selfishness and bad management, and then tried to take it from me in the divorce. Who would now spend the next twenty years in prison for drug trafficking.

It was hard to imagine choosing a worse partner than Lawrence.

My four children were the only reason I didn't regret marrying him with every fiber of my being. If I hadn't married Lawrence, I wouldn't have them.

They were worth it.

I cleaned up the few dishes I'd used and poured myself another glass of wine. Wandered into my quiet living room and sat on the corner of the couch. My kids had redecorated for me after I'd kicked out my ex. The colors were new, furniture moved, new photos on the walls. It felt more like my home again, after years of sharing it with him.

This place was filled with memories—both good and bad. I'd raised my children here. Cared for my parents here as their health declined. Lived a life here.

And now I lived here alone.

I put my wine glass down on the coffee table next to the latest mystery novel I'd been reading. Ben had brought it to me a few days ago. He'd started loaning me books recently. I'd mentioned in passing that I'd been looking for something to read, and the next day he'd stopped by with a book. I didn't usually read mysteries, but had decided to give it a try.

It had been riveting. I'd been glued to the page until the very end. After that, he'd suggested more books, and often brought new ones for me to borrow.

This one had a well-worn cover and dog-eared pages. I picked it up and traced my fingertip across the cover. Benjamin. I wondered what he was doing tonight. Was he sitting in his cabin up on the slope of the mountain, reading another book he'd bring me in a few days? Sipping a beer or a glass of whiskey? Or maybe a glass of wine—wine that I'd made?

Maybe I should call him. He lived alone, too. Was he lonely tonight?

Ben had been here at Salishan for over twenty-five years. I didn't know why he'd come, or much about where he'd been before. That wasn't something he'd ever shared with me. But I remembered the first time I'd met him, clear as day. I'd lost

Cooper—not for the first time, or the last. Ben had found him in the vineyard and brought him to me.

I hadn't known that day that Benjamin Gaines would one day be my oldest friend. Then, he'd just been a vineyard worker. One of many. But over the years, his role here had changed. He'd become the head groundskeeper and handyman. He built things, fixed things, planted gardens.

And now?

I sighed, thumbing through the pages. Now, he was a quiet presence in my life. The friend I knew I could always rely on. A man who cared deeply for my children. Who loved this land as much as I did.

But also a man who'd seen the worst moments of my life. Who knew the details of my past—the choices I'd made. He'd watched me stay married to Lawrence. Watched me try to hold my marriage together long after I should have let go. He'd been here through it all. The affairs. The ugly divorce.

I put the book down and picked up my wine. Took a sip. No, I wasn't going to call Ben. Not when I was feeling like this— so wanting and lonely. He was a good friend, and I was grateful to have him in my life. But the temptation of his rugged masculinity—his strength and steady presence—was too much of a risk. I couldn't imagine him seeing me as anything other than a longtime friend, and I wasn't going to allow myself to jeopardize that relationship.

I'd believed in love, once. In marriage vows and bonds that were meant to be forever. I wasn't sure what I believed, now. I believed in the love each of my children had found. Had faith they'd all chosen partners who would love and support them always.

But me? My time had come and gone. I'd lived a life with the wrong man. And I had other things now to make me happy.

Salishan was thriving. My children were happy. I had a beautiful grandson, another grandchild on the way, and certainly more to come.

I needed to learn to be content with that, no matter what my heart whispered about wanting more.

FOUR

BEN

I WASN'T ABOUT to admit it to anyone—especially Cooper and Chase—but I was nervous. Last night, sitting out in the dark watching my mattress burn, it had seemed so simple. Find Shannon—preferably alone—and ask her to dinner. I'd asked women on dates before, plenty of times. I may have had feelings for Shannon for a long time, but for most of those years, she'd been very unavailable. I'd pushed my feelings down—deep, deep down—and lived my life. That had included dating. I'd had relationships with several women over the years.

Of course, none of them had ever lasted, and I knew precisely why. None of them had been Shannon.

Still, I was no stranger to asking a woman out. In fact, I'd always considered myself rather good at it. But now that I was faced with asking Shannon Miles for a date, I found myself surprisingly anxious.

And busy. Cooper needed a hand out in the east vineyard, which took up most of the morning. Then Brynn called. One of the wine refrigerators in the Big House was making an odd noise. Turned out it was the compressor, but I was able to fix it. I went looking for Shannon after that, but she was busy in the lab. Spring was when she worked on her blends, mixing the grape varieties to produce different flavors. I didn't want to interrupt.

But as the day wore on, that nervous feeling in the pit of my stomach grew. Was Chase right? Had I been in the friend-zone for too long? Was I going to need to work harder to dig my way out?

Maybe I'd jumped the gun on burning that mattress.

Shannon and I *were* good friends. But I saw that as a positive—the basis for a strong relationship. I just needed the chance to show her that we could be so much more.

I had more work to do in one of the back gardens, so I spent the rest of my day out there. The air was fresh, the chill of winter finally receding. Made for a good day to be outside.

By the time my workday was over, I was dirty. And sweaty. I caught a glimpse of Shannon going into the Big House, but one look at my dirt-covered clothes and filthy hands, and I decided not to follow. I wasn't going to have the moment I asked her on our first date be marred by anything—particularly how I smelled.

Perhaps tomorrow.

THE NEXT DAY, I went down to Salishan full of resolve. Today was going to be the day I finally asked Shannon Miles on a date.

Before anyone could grab me to help with something, I went looking for her. She wasn't in her lab or the main cellar. I checked the bottling area, but she wasn't there, either.

The Big House was quiet—just a couple of employees in the kitchen prepping for the day. I went upstairs to check her office. She'd moved hers over from the old winery building some time ago. It was at the end of the hallway, next to a small conference room where Zoe often had consultations with clients.

I hesitated in the hall where I had a view through her half-open door. She was there, sitting at the vintage desk that had once been her father's. Her office was small but filled with natural light from the window behind her. She had photos of her family on a shelf and framed prints of different Salishan wines on the wall.

She sat with a pen in hand, leaning over a notebook. Her eyes flicked to her computer screen, then back to her paper. She wrote something, then her gaze went back to her computer.

So beautiful.

Her dark hair was streaked with silver, and she wore it back in a ponytail. She had a pair of reading glasses perched on her nose and her nails were painted a soft rose color. That was unusual for her. Brynn or Amelia—or both—had probably taken her for a manicure. That made me smile. Shannon didn't do enough for herself, and I knew spending time with the girls made her happy.

She tapped her pen against her lips. I gazed at her mouth, imagining those lips against mine. I'd been close enough to get a whiff of her hair a few times—she smelled like lavender—but what did she taste like? What would her breath feel like on my neck? Her naked body pressed against—

"Hey, Ben."

I nearly jumped out of my boots at the sound of Brynn's voice behind me. I cleared my throat, trying not to look too guilty. "Hi there, Sprout."

Her eyes flicked to her mother's partially open door, then back to me. "Are you okay?"

Damn. How long had I been standing here, staring? Fantasizing.

"Yes, fine. Just lost in thought for a minute, there."

"Okay. I just need to go talk to my mom." She jerked a thumb toward Shannon's office. "Did you need to see her about something? I can wait if—"

"No, you go right ahead." I couldn't very well say what I wanted to say to Shannon with her daughter standing a few feet away. Especially right after I'd been picturing Shannon naked. "I can wait."

Instead of loitering in the hallway, I went back downstairs while Brynn talked to her mom. I felt like I needed something to do, so I pretended to check on the wine fridge again. It was humming along nicely, but I gave it a once-over anyway.

I peeked out into the lobby and saw Brynn leave. Took a deep breath. Now was my chance.

"Ben," Roland said behind me. "I'm glad you're here. Do you have a minute?"

I swallowed back a frustrated growl. "Sure."

"We've been looking at options for upgrading the wine presses. I had Mom and Cooper take a look, but I wanted to get your opinion."

"Yeah, of course."

I followed Roland up to his office, casting a quick glance at Shannon before I went in. She looked up and for a second our eyes met. She gave me a quick smile, then went back to whatever she'd been working on.

God, that smile.

I sat down in Roland's office and we went over the equipment options. Even though I was anxious to speak to Shannon, I appreciated Roland including me on this decision. I wasn't the wine expert around here, but I'd been working on the winery's equipment for over twenty-five years. I knew a thing or two.

But my attention was half focused on the office down the hall. I was afraid I'd miss her—miss my chance to talk to her before she got busy.

"Thanks for your input," Roland said, turning his screen around. "The rep from the manufacturer will be out here next week if you want to talk to him."

"Good. I'll be around."

I tried not to look too eager to leave, but Roland's phone rang. I gave him a nod, which he returned, and ducked out into the hall.

Shannon was still in her office. My heart beat faster at the sight of her. I'd held back from her for so long. Kept my feelings buried deep. Now I was ready to explode like a fireworks show. Like I could walk right in there, pull her to her feet, push her up against the wall, and kiss the hell out of her.

She looked up and our eyes met again. I'd never once felt awkward around her, but right now, I felt as nervous as a boy about to ask a girl on a date for the very first time. Fifty-eight years old, and this woman made me feel like a shy kid again.

I nodded to her and approached her half-open door. "Morning."

"Good morning." She took her reading glasses off and set them on her desk. "What brings you up here?"

"Oh, the usual. Discussing wine presses with Roland."

Her eyes lit up. "That's going to make such a difference. The new one we're looking at is supposed to be so gentle. The lower pressure reduces oxidation. It's amazing."

"Sounds like it'll be an improvement."

"I think it will be," she said. "And it's such a relief to be in a place where we can consider new equipment. It seems like it wasn't that long ago we were wondering if we'd be able to stay in business."

I remembered that all too well. Her ex-husband had been the cause of it. "I'm glad those days are over."

"Me too."

We both paused for a few heartbeats, our eyes locked. Hers

were clear and blue, her eyelashes fluttering a little as she blinked.

"Shannon, I wanted to ask you—"

I faltered at the sound of a crying baby behind me.

Shannon looked past me, into the hallway. "Uh-oh. Can you excuse me for a second?"

Zoe was in Roland's doorway, holding Hudson up against her shoulder. She bounced and shifted her weight from one foot to the other. Hudson's cries filled the hall, her attempts to soothe him clearly failing.

I followed Shannon over to Roland's office.

"Aw, Huddy," Shannon said. "What's the matter?"

"Someone decided to get up at four o'clock this morning and refused to go back to sleep," Zoe said. "Now he's exhausted."

"Isn't Marina watching him today?" Shannon asked.

"She just called," Zoe said, continuing her bounce-sway-pat routine to no avail. "She had a family emergency and has to go out of town for a few days. I figured she was just running late, and we have a luncheon at eleven, so I brought him with me. I thought she could pick him up here, but she's on her way to Portland."

"I'll take him home," Roland said.

Shannon reached for him. "I can take him."

"Are you sure?" Roland asked.

"Of course," she said. "I know how busy you are."

"I'll come home after the luncheon's over," Zoe said. "It should only last a couple of hours."

"That's fine," Shannon said as Zoe handed a crying Hudson to her. "I'll get him down for a nap and he'll be good as new."

"Thank you so much," Zoe said, draping her diaper bag strap over Shannon's shoulder. "You're a lifesaver."

"Thanks, Mom," Roland said.

"Come on, mister. Let's go home and take a nice nap." She

glanced at me. "Sorry, Benjamin. Did you have something you needed to ask me?"

Not in front of two of your kids while you're holding a crying baby. "Oh, no. You go on and get that little one home."

She smiled, rubbing Hudson's back. "Okay. Zoe, take your time. We'll be fine."

"Thank you again," Zoe said, straightening her blouse.

I watched Shannon take Hudson downstairs. Heard his cries disappear as they left the building.

Damn.

That hadn't worked out the way I'd wanted. I'd just have to try again later.

FIVE

SHANNON

THE TASTING ROOM WAS EMPTY. It was a quiet evening, so I'd sent Brynn home early. Now, ten minutes to closing, I didn't expect we'd get any more customers.

I'd spent my morning with Hudson, although he'd slept through most of it. Poor little nugget had been so exhausted he'd taken a three-and-a-half-hour nap. I'd fed him lunch and he'd been back to his happy self. Zoe had come home soon after, so I'd gone back to work.

The afternoon had gotten away from me, and the next thing I knew, it was nearly seven. My days were like that more often than not—filled with work and family. Life was busy.

Which was why I'd been looking forward to tonight.

I got out two wine glasses and set them on the bar. After mulling it over for a minute or two, I chose a wine—a sweet red blend with a hint of blackberry. We aged it in bourbon barrels, sourced from a local distillery, giving it a smooth finish. It had become one of my favorites.

My friend Naomi came in, dressed in a beige trench coat. Her blond hair was cut short—about chin length—and she had a handbag slung over her shoulder.

Naomi Harris and I were perhaps the unlikeliest of friends. She'd been my husband's mistress, years ago. Borne him two children, both while he was married to me. I hadn't known at the time. More importantly, Naomi hadn't known about me. She'd believed Lawrence to be single. She'd been devastated to discover he had a wife and children, living just half an hour away.

At first, I'd wanted nothing to do with her. I'd felt sympathy for her children, and hadn't wanted to get in the way of them getting to know their half-siblings. But eventually, I'd decided I needed to clear the air with Naomi.

We'd sat down together over coffee and told each other our stories. That day, I'd come to an important realization: Naomi and I were both victims. We'd been deeply wounded by the same man, and neither of us had ever intended to hurt the other.

After that, we'd cautiously begun to form a friendship. We'd bonded over our shared experiences as women and mothers, as well as our hatred of the man who'd betrayed us both.

Lawrence had gotten prison. I'd gotten a friend. Yet another way I'd come out far ahead, despite all the horrible things he'd done.

"Hi, Shannon," Naomi said with a smile. She put her handbag on the bar and took off her coat. "How was your day?"

"Busy," I said and poured us each a glass, then re-corked the bottle. I pushed her glass toward her, then went around the bar to take a seat next to her. "Emergency babysitting duties this morning, catching up with work all afternoon. How about you?"

She swirled her wine. "Busy. Elijah dropped his project in a puddle on the way to school. Then he was upset about being late. Poor buddy."

"Where is he tonight?"

"With the family next door," she said.

"I'm glad you could get away." I lifted my glass and took a sip. "I haven't seen you in a while. What's new?"

She took a drink of her wine before answering. "Well... I'm dating someone."

I gasped and sat up a little straighter. "You are? Tell me."

"His name is Jack Cordero. I've known him for several years, but just as an acquaintance, really. He asked me to dinner a few weeks ago. I was so surprised I spilled water all over him. It was embarrassing."

"Oh no," I said, laughing.

"Not my finest moment. But even after that, he still wanted to go out. And we've seen each other almost every day since."

"That's wonderful," I said. "What does he do?"

"He's a cop. He spent most of his career with the Seattle police department. He was married once before, but they never had children. They divorced eleven years ago. Obviously, I checked. Then, a few years ago, he moved out here."

"I'm so happy for you."

"Thanks," she said. "I'm not getting ahead of myself. It's early. But I like him a lot. I haven't introduced him to Elijah yet, but Grace knows him. She gave him her stamp of approval."

"Good. That's important."

"It is," she said. "If this ends up going somewhere, my kids need to be okay with it. More than okay with it. But... I don't know, Shannon, I have a feeling about him."

I took another sip of wine. "I think it's wonderful."

She took a drink, then held up her glass. "This is so good. You have a gift."

"Thank you."

"What about you?" she asked, setting her glass down. "Have you thought about dating?"

I laughed softly. "Me? No."

"Why not?"

"How much time do you have? It's a long list."

She sighed. "Shannon."

"My *kids* aren't even dating anymore," I said. "Not really."

"What does that have to do with anything?" she asked. "Don't tell me you're too old."

"I am too old."

She rolled her eyes. "Hardly."

"I'm fifty-seven. Who starts dating again at that age?"

"Lots of people," she said.

It was my turn to roll my eyes. "Do you know how long it's been since I *dated*? I got married when I was twenty-two."

"All the more reason for you to at least be open to the possibility."

I took a sip. "I just feel like that part of my life is over. I got married and raised a family. Now my kids are starting families and I'm busy here."

"I'm not saying there's anything wrong with staying single if you're happy," she said. "And heaven knows being single is better than being with the wrong man."

"Cheers to that." I raised my glass and she clinked hers against it.

"But don't assume your life is over. You're a beautiful, vibrant woman. A good man could make you very happy, in all sorts of ways." She winked.

I almost choked on my wine. "All sorts of ways?"

"Sure. You remember sex, right?"

"Vaguely."

"It's been a long time for me, too," she said.

Yet another thing we had in common, and for the same reason.

"I can't even remember the last time," I said. "Not for sure. I kicked him out almost two years ago. But even then, it had been years."

"He was failing you in every way," she said.

"He was. I think the worst part is that I blamed myself. I thought maybe after four children, he didn't find me attractive anymore."

"Shannon, I'm so sorry, I—"

"No," I said, putting up a hand to stop her. "Don't. It's not your fault."

She nodded.

I grabbed the bottle and refilled both our glasses. "Now that you're dating, does it make you nervous? The idea of having sex again?"

"A little," she said. "But it's exciting, too. Being with Jack reminds me that I'm more than a mother. I'm still a woman. I want to explore that."

"Good for you."

"You know, after Elijah, I felt a bit like you do now. Like that part of my life was over. How would I meet someone? And if I did, would they want to date a single mother? I figured a relationship wasn't in the cards for me. But the moment Jack asked me to dinner, I realized my life wasn't over."

I was happy for Naomi. Happy that she was moving forward with her life. She was younger than me. She still had plenty of time to create her version of forever.

My situation was different. My life was different. And it was fine.

So why did I feel a hint of jealousy?

"Oh, hi ladies," Zoe said from the doorway. Her dark hair was down and the tiny stud in her nose sparkled. "Sorry to interrupt. I was upstairs catching up on a few things and I heard voices."

"Hi, Zoe," Naomi said. "Care to have a glass of wine with us?"

"Gladly," Zoe said.

I motioned for us to move to a table. While they took their seats, I got another glass and poured, then sat at the table with them.

"Thank you." Zoe lifted her glass. "What should we toast to?"

"To being passionate, sensual women," Naomi said, smiling at me.

"I can definitely toast to that," Zoe said, and we all clinked our glasses. "Is there something you need to share with the class, Shannon?"

"No, but Naomi recently started dating someone."

"Congratulations," Zoe said, raising her glass again. "You certainly deserve a good man."

"Thank you," Naomi said with a smile. "I agree."

Zoe tilted her head and looked at me, blinking a few times.

"What?" I asked.

"I'm just wondering when you're going to wake up and realize that you deserve a good man, too."

"Zoe Miles, we've had this conversation," I said. "You know how I feel about it."

"But how do you feel about *him*?"

"Him?" Naomi asked, her eyebrows lifting. "Him, who?"

Zoe pursed her lips and blinked at me again.

"We're good friends," I said. "That's all."

"Mm-hmm," Zoe said.

"Oh, I know who you're talking about," Naomi said, lowering her voice. "Shannon, you didn't tell me you had a thing for Ben."

"What makes you think I do?"

Zoe snorted.

"Why wouldn't you?" Naomi asked. "He's handsome and sweet. And he obviously likes you."

"As I said, he's a good friend."

Zoe put her hand over mine. "Shannon, you're a very smart woman, but you've been out of the game too long. That man does not like you *as a friend*."

Feeling suddenly flustered—why was my heart beating so hard?—I took a drink so I wouldn't have to reply. What could I say to that? Ben was a friend, and it was silly of me to hope for more.

Was that what this feeling was? This fluttering in my stomach and warmth in my cheeks? Was this *hope*?

"You're blushing and don't blame the wine," Zoe said. "Come on, Shannon. You know you want that big rugged man between your legs."

"Zoe!"

She laughed. "What? Don't give me that *I'm too old* line. You're not. If I have to give up sex when I'm fifty-seven, I'm going to be pissed."

"I realize I'm not too old to sleep with someone. Everything still works. But it's more complicated than that."

"It doesn't have to be," Zoe said.

"You could start slow," Naomi said. "Besides, there's a lot we missed out on when we were younger."

"Like what?" I asked.

"Sexting," Naomi said.

Zoe nodded. "Oh, yeah."

"Sexting?"

"Yeah, sexting is when you and—"

"I know," I said, putting a hand up to stop Zoe from giving me the definition. "I'm aware of what sexting is."

"But you've never done it," Naomi said. "Sexy texts can be really fun."

I wasn't about to admit it to these two, but I did feel like I'd missed out on a few things. Sexy texts did sound fun.

"I know what you need," Zoe said.

I eyed her for a second. "I'm afraid to even ask."

Naomi sipped her wine, looking amused.

"A spa day," Zoe said.

"You think I need a *spa day*?"

She nodded. "Some skin treatments, maybe a massage. A wax. Things to make you feel pretty and ready to get naked."

"A wax?" I asked. "Do I really need a wax to get naked with someone?"

Naomi shrugged. "I started waxing. It's very nice."

"I'm not cut out for this."

"Relax," Zoe said. "You don't have to get a wax to get naked with Ben. He'll be into you no matter what. Besides, if I had to guess, I'd bet he's a fan of the natural look. Just trim it up a little and you'll be fine. Viva la bush."

"I can't believe I'm having this conversation with you."

Zoe grinned.

"And I'm not getting naked with anyone," I said. "Especially Benjamin."

"See, right there," Zoe said, pointing at me with her wine. "You always call him by his full name. You're the only one who does. You realize that, don't you?"

"The first time we met, he introduced himself as Benjamin," I said. "So yes, I've always called him that. What's your point?"

"That there's something between you two," Zoe said. "And it's okay if you stop denying it."

I wanted to tell her that I wasn't denying anything. But that would have been a lie. I'd been denying my feelings for Ben for a long time.

"I wouldn't know where to begin," I said, my voice soft. "It's literally been decades since I dated. I feel like I've lived a lifetime since then and everything is different. I'm different. I'm older, I've had four children, been through a horrible divorce. Those things left their mark."

"All right, I'll stop pushing," Zoe said. "But if you want to take me up on that spa day, just let me know."

"Thanks."

Zoe took another drink, smiling at me from behind her glass. Naomi had a similar look in her eyes. They were being absurd. Ben wasn't interested in dating me, so I certainly didn't need to be concerned about things like waxing.

Did I?

SIX

BEN

VOICES CAUGHT MY ATTENTION. I'd come into the Big House through the kitchen to put some things away in one of the storerooms. Was someone in the tasting room? The winery was closed, but it sounded like it might be Shannon and Zoe.

I hadn't seen Shannon all day—not since this morning when my attempt to ask her to dinner had gone sideways. If she was on her way out, now might be a good time to try again. I glanced down at my clothes to make sure they were sufficiently clean—they were—and took a deep breath.

Laughter spilled out from the tasting room. It sounded like more than just Shannon and Zoe. Naomi Harris, if I wasn't mistaken. That made me smile. Who other than Shannon Miles would find friendship as a result of her ex-husband's infidelity?

But if Naomi was here, Shannon was probably going to stay and visit with her for a while. Now wasn't the time. I'd go home and see her tomorr—

"And I'm not getting naked with anyone," Shannon said. "Especially Benjamin."

I stopped in my tracks. What had she just said?

"See, right there." That was Zoe. "You always call him by his first name. You're the only one who does that. You realize that, don't you?"

It was true. She did. I loved hearing her call me Benjamin. Always had.

"The first time we met, he introduced himself as Benjamin," Shannon said. Also true; I remembered it well. "So yes, I've always called him that. What's your point?"

"That there's something between you two," Zoe said. "And it's okay if you stop denying it."

I held my breath, knowing I wasn't meant to hear this conversation. And yet, unable to walk away.

"I wouldn't know where to begin." Shannon's voice had quieted. "It's literally been decades since I dated. I feel like I've lived a lifetime since then and everything is different. I'm different. I'm older, I've had four children, been through a horrible divorce. Those things left their mark."

"All right, I'll stop pushing," Zoe said. "But if you want to take me up on that spa day, just let me know."

"Thanks."

I closed my eyes, putting a hand on my chest. *Oh, Shannon.* The pain in her voice gutted me. Was that really what she thought? That the possibility of love didn't exist for her anymore?

Moving quietly, I left through the kitchen so she wouldn't know I'd been there. I felt bad for listening—I hadn't meant to eavesdrop, but she'd said the words *naked* and *Benjamin* in close proximity. Who could blame me?

This wasn't going to be as simple as I'd thought. When I'd imagined asking her to dinner, I'd never considered the possibility that she'd say no. And what had she meant when she'd said she wasn't getting naked with anyone, *especially Benjamin*?

Maybe I'd been reading her wrong. Did she see me as a

good friend, and nothing more? Or was Zoe right, and Shannon was denying what had been quietly forming between us?

I didn't know.

So I went on home, unsure as to how I should handle this. For a second, I wondered if I ought to take Cooper and Chase up on their offer to help. But I dismissed that idea quickly. No, those boys would mean well, but they'd only wind up getting me in trouble somehow.

Back at home, I stood looking out my front window. At the view of Salishan's vineyards. The winery. Shannon's house. I could see it all from here.

The view was why I'd bought the place, years ago.

I wasn't sure what I was going to do about Shannon. I'd been patient for a long time. If I needed to, I could wait a bit longer. But suddenly my simple plan seemed short-sighted. If she wasn't sure about dating—and there was that comment about not getting naked with me that I really needed to figure out—maybe I should take a different approach.

But I didn't know what.

THE NEXT MORNING, I wasn't any closer to figuring out my next move. I went to work and spent my first couple of hours avoiding Cooper. I didn't want him asking awkward questions. And there was no doubt he would.

What I needed was another perspective. Someone who could give me a little insight. But who?

I wasn't about to talk to her kids. *How can I coax your mother into dating me, and by the way, do you think she meant what she said about not wanting to get naked with me* was not something I could ask any of them. Even Cooper.

Especially Cooper.

If I knew Naomi better, I might be able to talk to her. We'd met a few times. But I didn't know her well enough to ask about Shannon. Not like this.

Which left just one person—someone I knew I could trust to both be discreet and tell me the truth.

Zoe.

Their mother and daughter-in-law dynamic was just outside the realm of mother-child—enough that I figured I could ask Zoe for a little advice without it being too awkward. And Zoe was straightforward—something I'd always appreciated about her. She wouldn't bullshit me, and she knew Shannon as well as —or better than—anyone around here.

I found her in the event room in the Big House, directing employees who were setting up for a wedding. I made eye contact and nodded, then waited with my hands in my pockets while she finished up.

She flipped through a few pages on a clipboard, then walked over to me. "Hey, Ben. What's up?"

"Do you have a minute?"

"Sure."

I hesitated while she looked at me expectantly. The employees buzzed around the room, stringing up lights and moving chairs. "Can we go outside? It's personal."

"Yeah, of course."

We went out through the kitchen into the early spring air. It smelled like honeysuckle and pine.

I rubbed my beard and cleared my throat. "I need some advice."

Her eyebrows twitched upward. "About what?"

"Shannon."

She held the clipboard against her chest and smiled. "Okay."

I figured the best thing to do was be honest. "I overheard a few things last night when you were talking in the tasting room. I didn't mean to, and it wasn't much, but..."

"Oh, shit."

"I know."

"What did you hear, exactly?" she asked.

"Mostly just the part about how long it's been since she's dated, and how everything is different now."

"And?" she asked, raising her eyebrows again.

"And something about not getting naked with anyone, especially me." I put a hand up. "But we don't need to talk about the naked part."

She laughed. "Fair enough. But for the record, she didn't mean it."

I paused for a beat, my mouth half open. "You don't think so?"

"Definitely not," she said. "Since we're not talking about it, I won't tell you that she's totally lying to herself and she absolutely wants to get naked with you."

I cleared my throat again. "Anyway. I've been thinking I'd like to ask her out."

"Oh my god, finally," she said. "What the hell's taken you so long?"

"Oh, I don't know, the fact that up until recently, she was legally married?"

Zoe waved her hand. "Whatever. It's probably best that you haven't made a move yet anyway."

"Why?"

"Well, you heard her. She's really nervous about the idea of dating again. I think she's actually convinced herself that she can't. That living in that big house by herself, making wine, and doting on her grandkids is her life now."

"That's what I'm afraid of. Yesterday I thought I'd just get her alone for a few minutes and ask her to dinner. What could be simpler than that? But now I'm not so sure. I've waited a long time for this. I'd like to go into it with a little more confidence that the answer's going to be yes."

Zoe tapped her fingers on the back of her other arm. "Ordinarily, I'd say you're being too cautious, and you should just go for it. But in this case, I think Shannon might need a little more coaxing. Get her used to the idea that you're pursuing her before you ask her for an actual date."

"All right," I said. "I can do that."

"Just don't wait too long," she said. "Not just for her sake—for yours too. You have the patience of a saint, Ben. I honestly don't know how you've done it."

I smiled. "The right woman is worth the wait."

"That," she said, gesturing at me. "Whatever that was just now? Use that. It'll be irresistible."

"So, ease her into it?" I asked.

"Yes. Just a nudge. Think of it like... dating foreplay. She's been watching from the sidelines for a really long time."

"That she has. Thanks, Zoe."

"Anytime," she said.

I walked away, pondering what Zoe had said, and what I'd heard Shannon say last night. I understood the real meaning behind Shannon's words. She didn't see herself as desirable anymore, and she questioned whether someone would want her after everything she'd been through.

Shannon. Beautiful Shannon. You can't imagine how much I want you.

Zoe was right, Shannon needed a little coaxing. Especially because *dating* her wasn't my endgame. I wanted much more than that. I'd loved this woman from afar for a long time. A date with her was only the beginning—the beginning of forever, if I had anything to say about it.

I was a patient man and I was going to coax Shannon Miles right into my arms.

SEVEN

SHANNON

SOMEONE HAD DELIVERED flowers to the wrong office.

The bouquet sitting on my desk was beautiful—a mix of red roses, lilies, pink dianthus, and heather. And the scent was lovely, the floral aroma filling the air. But there was no card, so I didn't know who it belonged to.

I went downstairs and found Lindsey in the lobby. "Did you talk to the floral delivery person?"

Her eyebrows drew together. "No. I didn't see anyone."

"Someone delivered flowers, but they put them in my office by mistake," I said. "I'm assuming they're for Jamie or Zoe."

"I'm not sure," she said.

"That's okay. I'll ask Roland if he sent them. Actually, I'll congratulate him if he did. They're gorgeous, and what a sweet thing to do."

I went back upstairs. Roland wasn't in the office yet, so I sent him a text.

Me: Did you send Zoe flowers?

Roland: No, why?

That was odd.

Me: There are flowers on my desk but no card. The delivery person put them in the wrong place. I thought they might be for Zoe.

Roland: It wasn't me. But why do you think they're in the wrong place?

Me: They're not for me.

Roland: How do you know?

Me: Who would send me flowers?

Roland: I don't know, but if they're on your desk...

Me: I'll see if I can find the card.

My office smelled wonderful. It was too bad I couldn't keep them. I wondered if this meant Jamie was seeing someone. She was our other events person, and as far as I knew, she was single. But perhaps she'd started dating someone. Whoever he was, he knew how to pick a lovely flower arrangement.

I checked around the vase again, but didn't see a card. It wasn't tucked in among the blooms either.

Finally, I found a little white envelope on the floor beneath my desk. I must have knocked it over when I'd gotten here—maybe when I'd taken off my coat. I picked it up, but there was no name on the outside. Just a little stamp with the florist's logo.

I popped open the envelope and took out the crisp white card. Inside was one word, written in black ink. *Shannon.*

I stared at my name, penned in neat handwriting. The flowers were for *me?*

Turning the card over, I looked for another name. Peeked in the envelope in case I'd missed something. But there was no other signature. No indication who'd sent them.

Were they from one of my kids? It wasn't my birthday. It wasn't the anniversary of Salishan's founding or any other milestone I could recall. We'd already celebrated my divorce. Why would one of them have sent me flowers?

Roland obviously hadn't. He would have told me when I'd texted him. It wasn't Cooper. He'd have bypassed a florist and made the arrangement himself. Could it have been Leo? Or Brynn? They didn't seem likely either.

And these flowers weren't the sort of thing someone would send their mother. They weren't send-to-a-friend flowers, either, so I doubted it had been Naomi. A professional contact was possible—perhaps one of our vendors or a winery client. But they would have sent a more detailed note—and probably chosen a more business-appropriate arrangement.

These flowers weren't friendly. They were romantic.

"Those are pretty." Zoe's voice behind me made me jump.

I put my hand to my chest. "You startled me. And yes, they are."

"Sorry, I didn't mean to scare you." Her eyes flicked to the flowers. "Who sent them?"

"I don't know." I narrowed my eyes. "But why do I think you do?"

She shrugged. "I don't know."

I wasn't sure if she was saying she didn't know who'd sent the flowers, or she didn't know why I thought she knew.

"Zoe Miles, are you hiding something from me?"

"I didn't send you the flowers," she said.

"That's not what I asked."

She held up her wrist and looked down at it, but she wasn't wearing a watch. "Look at the time. We have a wedding tonight, I need to get to work."

I put my hands on my hips, but she turned and walked away. She did know something, which meant it had to be...

But he couldn't have. Could he? It had to be a mistake.

And yet, the card said my name.

I had an unfamiliar fluttering in my tummy—a feeling I hadn't experienced in years. Tracing my finger over the letters of my name, I dared to think it. Dared to let his name drift through my mind.

Had Benjamin Gaines sent me flowers?

The thought that it had been him left me a little breathless, and strangely giddy. I realized I was smiling, the card with my name dangling from my fingertips. I took a deep breath, inhaling the flowers' fragrance. So beautiful. So thoughtful.

And it occurred to me in that moment how much I wanted it to be him.

Over the next few hours, I didn't get much work done. I kept stopping to gaze at the flowers or getting up to peek downstairs to see if Ben was here.

I wondered if I should call him to say thank you. But what if he hadn't sent the flowers? That would be awkward. And if he had sent them, why hadn't he signed his name? Had the florist made a mistake, or had he done that on purpose?

Around noon I gave up trying to work and decided to go home for lunch. I left the flowers on my desk, shouldered my purse, and went downstairs.

The lobby was quiet, although it would get busier later when wedding guests arrived. I went out through the kitchen, where the caterer was already prepping for tonight's event.

Outside was sunny and pleasant, the early spring air fragrant. A familiar voice caught my attention. Pausing, I glanced over my shoulder into the back garden.

Ben stood speaking to Roland. He pointed at one of the pear trees and said something I couldn't quite hear. Roland nodded. Then Ben's eyes moved to mine, our gazes locking. One corner of his mouth hooked upward in a small smile, and he winked at me.

My breath caught in my throat, a rush of nerves made my stomach flutter, and my cheeks flushed. Ben went back to his conversation with Roland. But that look. That wink. He'd never winked at me before.

Oh my god, he *had* sent me the flowers.

I went home, my entire body tingling. It seemed so silly that a bouquet and a wink could have such an effect on me. I wasn't a naive little girl anymore. But that look he'd given me. Full of heat and a little mischief, like we shared a secret.

I didn't see him for the rest of the day. When I went home that night, I decided to text him a thank you.

Me: Do I have you to thank for the flowers?

Ben: Yes. Did you like them?

Me: They're beautiful. Thank you.

Ben: My pleasure.

Me: It's been a long time since a man bought me flowers.

Ben: Thought so. Figured it was time to change that.

Me: Why didn't you sign your name? Was it supposed to be a secret?

Ben: Not really. Just having a little fun with you.

I laughed and bit my lower lip. Was he flirting with me? It had been so long, I wasn't sure if I'd recognize it.

Me: Thank you again. That was really sweet.

Ben: You're welcome. Good night, Shannon.

Me: Good night, Benjamin.

THE NEXT MORNING, I opened my front door and found a large package on my doorstep. It was wrapped in brown paper and tied with twine. No shipping label or address. Just a tag hanging from the twine, my name written in neat handwriting.

Ben's handwriting.

Feeling a little jumpy with excitement, I brought it inside and set it on the dining table. I untied the package and tore it open. Careful not to spill the foam packing material, I dug through the box.

I felt something hard and smooth, like glass. A glass bottle, perhaps. Had he sent me wine? That was odd.

I pulled out what was indeed a wine bottle. One of ours, in fact. But it was empty. He'd cut off the bottom of the bottle and run a chain through the top with a metal circle at the base of the neck to hold it in place. Hanging from the circle—inside the bottle—was a votive holder with a candle.

It was beautiful.

Inside the box were two more just like it. They'd look wonderful hanging on my front porch.

I checked the box to see if there was anything else. Perhaps a note or a card. I found another bottle—this one wrapped in bubble wrap. It was heavier than the lanterns had been.

I unwrapped the bottle—it was unopened—and stared at the label. I hadn't seen one of these in years. It was a Salishan wine, but the label was old and faded. The date was twenty-six years ago.

The year Ben had come to work for Salishan.

I ran my thumb along the label. It brought back a whirlwind of memories. My boys had been so little. Brynn hadn't even been born. I remembered that summer so well. Remembered meeting Ben for the first time when he'd found Cooper in the vineyard.

Where had he found this? Had he kept a bottle from his first year working at the winery?

It was a Saturday—Ben's day off—which meant I probably wouldn't see him. So I decided to call.

"Good morning," he said.

"Morning. I see you've been out and about early today."

"I take it you opened your front door?"

I laughed. "I did. Thank you. I don't know what to say."

"You're welcome. I can come by sometime and hang the lanterns if you want."

"Please do," I said. "I think they'll look lovely on the porch. Where did you get the wine?"

"I had it at home," he said.

"It's from your first season here, isn't it?"

"I'm pleased you remember."

"Of course I do." I nibbled on my bottom lip, unsure of what else to say. "Well, I won't keep you. I just wanted to say thanks."

"You're welcome," he said. "I'll see you later."

"Okay."

I ended the call and put my phone down. This was so unexpected. Flowers, and now this? A gift he'd made, and a sweet reminder of the first time we'd met?

What are you up to, Benjamin Gaines?

EIGHT

SHANNON

BEN'S GIFTS didn't end there. The next day, I had another package on my porch. This time it was a new mug. It was white and said *Good Morning, Beautiful* in gold letters.

I stared at it for a while before making my morning tea. Traced my fingers over the words. Was he really calling me beautiful?

After brewing my tea, I sent him a picture of the mug.

Ben: That's nice. Who sent it to you?

Me: Stop. Wait, didn't you?

Ben: I'm teasing, it was me. Do you like it?

Me: I love it. Very pretty.

Ben: So are you.

My heart did a little flutter and I couldn't contain my smile.

Me: Thank you. This is so sweet.

Ben: You're welcome. Can I come by later? I can hang those lanterns for you.

Me: I'd love that.

Ben: Great, I'll see you this afternoon.

I put my phone down and took a sip of my tea. This afternoon couldn't come soon enough.

THE KNOCK on my door gave me butterflies. I'd never felt nervous to see Ben before. Not really. We'd been friends for years, and close friends since my ex had left. But now, something was happening between us. He'd sent me flowers and thoughtful gifts. He'd called me *beautiful*.

There was no denying that he was an intensely attractive man. From his tanned skin and salt-and-pepper beard to his thick arms and strong hands, he was handsome and capable.

Was he actually interested in me?

I answered the door, expecting to see Ben. I blinked in surprise to see Leo and Hannah on my front porch. Leo had his arm around her shoulders—his scarred arm, no less.

I wanted to hug Hannah every time I saw her. Because of her, my son had life in his eyes—such a contrast from the wounded young man who'd come home to us. Although I'd been as shocked as anyone to hear they were having a baby, I couldn't wait to meet my granddaughter in a few months.

"Hey, Mom," Leo said. He was holding my stand mixer. "We just wanted to return this."

"Thanks." I moved aside so they could come in. "You can just set it on the counter."

Leo took the mixer into the kitchen while Hannah came in and sat at the dining table.

"Thanks again for letting me use it," she said. "I definitely need to get one for myself. That lemon meringue pie recipe you gave me is amazing."

"Oh good, I'm glad it turned out. Would you like tea?"

"Sure, thanks."

I went into the kitchen and put the kettle on, then brought mugs and a little basket of tea bags to the dining table.

The front door swung open and Cooper sauntered in. Amelia was with him—of course—her hand clasped in his. My son had what you might call a passion for funny boyfriend t-shirts. Today, he wore a shirt that said *If You Think I'm Cute, You Should See My Girlfriend*. It was probably the Cooper-est shirt I'd ever seen.

"Mominator," Cooper said. He dropped Amelia's hand long enough to give me a hug.

"Hey, Cooper," I said, hugging him back. Then I hugged Amelia, too. "What are you up to?"

"Not much." He slid onto the bench at the dining table and pulled Amelia onto his lap. "What about you?"

His eyes flicked to the kitchen, and I had a pretty good idea of what had brought him here. I'd made scones earlier. Cooper had a sixth sense when it came to my baking.

"I made scones this morning," I said. "Would you like some?"

"Heck, yes," Cooper said.

Amelia patted him on the cheek, then stood. "I'll help."

She and I brought out the scones, along with butter and jam, as well as more mugs for tea.

Brynn and Chase seemed to appear out of nowhere and the next thing I knew, my dining table was filled with my kids. I glanced at the door a few times, wondering if Roland and Zoe were going to show up next.

I sat with a mug of tea and listened while they chatted—even Leo. Not only did Leo contribute to the conversation, he smiled *and laughed.*

These people made my heart so full.

There was another knock on the door and Cooper sprang up to answer it.

"Ben," he said as he opened the door. "Good to see you, man. Come in."

My throat felt tight, like I wasn't going to be able to speak. I hadn't said a word to my kids about Ben's flowers or other gifts. And I hadn't anticipated having an audience when he came over today.

Judging by the surprise on his face, he hadn't counted on my kids being here, either.

"Shannon," he said, nodding to me.

I rose from my seat and gestured to the kitchen. He followed me in.

"Hi," I said. "Thanks for stopping by."

"I brought you something." He held out a hardbound book. "I borrowed it from the library, but it was so good I thought you might want to read it."

"Thank you," I said, taking the book and holding it against my chest. "I just finished the last one you loaned me, so this is perfect timing."

Laughter spilled into the kitchen from the other room. His eyes darted to the doorway, then back to me.

"How about I hang those lanterns for you?"

"That would be great."

I glanced at my kids, still sitting around my dining table, as I helped Ben get the lanterns. I loved that they still came over—and that they felt like this house was still a home to them. But for the first time, I kind of wished they hadn't stayed.

Feeling a little guilty for that thought, I took the lanterns out to the front porch.

Ben spent some time hanging them while I sat nearby and watched him work. Watched his capable hands as he used his tools. His strong body as he stretched to reach the beam and drilled hooks into place.

"How does this look?" he asked when he'd finished.

The lanterns hung at differing heights, the light catching on the glass. "They're perfect."

Our eyes met and he held my gaze for a long moment. The heat in his subtle smile sent a shiver down my spine.

The sound of laughter inside jolted me from my daze.

"I should probably get home," Ben said.

A little wave of disappointment washed over me. Should I invite him to stay? What would it mean if I did?

I was feeling things—big things—and it scared me. I'd told myself more times than I could count that Ben and I were just friends. That I wasn't going to date again. That my life was fine the way it was. And the idea of things changing between us made me more than a little bit nervous. So I hesitated.

He closed his toolbox and picked it up. His eyes made a slow, deliberate trip down my body, then up again. "I'll see you later, Shannon."

"Bye, Benjamin."

I went back inside and sat with my kids at the table. Eventually, the impromptu gathering tapered off. Two by two, they left, until it was once again just me, alone in my house.

IT WAS LATE, but I couldn't sleep. Instead of continuing to toss and turn, I went out to my front porch and lit the candles in the lanterns Ben had made. I sat in the wooden chair wrapped in a sweater, the book he'd brought in my lap. The candlelight flickered, casting shadows across the porch. I decided I'd read a while and hopefully get sleepy.

Before I'd gotten more than a few pages into the book, I got a text.

Ben: Any chance you're awake?

Me: I am. Couldn't sleep.

Ben: Me neither. Did you light the candles tonight?

Me: I did. They're beautiful.

Ben: Glad you like them. What are you doing now?

Me: Sitting on the porch with the book you brought me. Sorry if you wanted to talk earlier. The kids all just wandered over.

Ben: Can't say I blame them. You did have scones.

Me: True. Those are hard to resist.

Ben: Mm, so hard to resist.

I bit my lip and read his last text several times. Was he talking about the scones? Of course he was talking about the scones. I was a good cook. He obviously wasn't saying *I* was hard to resist.

Was he?

Me: Are we still talking about scones?

Ben: Maybe. You have quite a few things that are hard to resist.

Me: I do?

Ben: Oh, Shannon. If you only knew.

My heart fluttered and that sense of giddiness stole through me again. Texting him like this, late at night, made me feel a little bit brave. Brave enough to...

Me: Tell me.

Ben: I've had to resist you for a long time. Resist your eyes. Your smile.

Ben: And those lips. I'd die a happy man if I could taste them even once.

Me: It's been a long time since these lips have been kissed.

Ben: Too long. Far too long.

Ben: Shannon, I'd kiss you so you'd forget ever having been kissed before.

Me: It would feel good, wouldn't it?

Ben: So good. I'd put my hands in your hair and kiss you breathless. Remind you what it feels like to be desired.

Me: It's been such a long time since I felt that, too.

Ben: Shannon, you're the most beautiful woman I've ever known. If you have any doubts that you're desirable, I'd love to be the man to fix that for you.

Me: It's hard not to have doubts. This body is... well, it's not the same. And I haven't... in a long time.

Ben: There are so many things to love about your body. And if you let me, I'll show you each and every one. But the most important thing is that it's *you*.

Ben: I find *you* desirable, Shannon. All of you.

I closed my eyes, imagining Ben's lips against mine. His hands on my body. I'd been trying to tell myself I had plenty of things to fulfill me. That I didn't need anything—or anyone —else.

But what if I did want more?

Me: Benjamin?

Ben: Yes?

Me: You're desirable, too. In fact, I think you might be the sexiest man I've ever seen.

Ben: I'm a little bit speechless.

Me: You are. So sexy. So handsome and strong. Can I tell you something else?

Ben: Oh my darling, please do.

Me: I imagine it sometimes... what it would feel like to kiss you.

Ben: Tell me.

Me: I imagine the way your beard would feel on my face. And what it would be like to have your arms around me. Your hands touching me.

Ben: Believe me, I've imagined the same things. And more.

Me: I've imagined more, too. Is this really happening? Are we...?

Ben: Yes. How does that make you feel?

I took a few breaths of the cool night air. My cheeks were warm, my body lighting up in ways I hadn't experienced in a long time. How *did* this make me feel?

Me: Honestly? A little bit scared.

Ben: That's okay. We don't have to rush. But the next time I see you, I am going to kiss you.

I thought about telling him to come over and kiss me now. But I stopped before I typed the words. I did want Ben's kiss—and so much more. But it was easy to imagine while I sat here alone in the dark. It was quite another thing to invite him here in the middle of the night.

I wasn't sure I was ready for that. Not because I was innocent or naive. I had different reasons for hesitating—reasons that were no less real.

It felt like opening a book I'd thought I'd lost long ago. Still familiar, but I needed to keep turning the pages to reacquaint myself with the story before I was ready for the climax.

Me: If you do, maybe I'll kiss you back.

Ben: Maybe? Not sure about those odds, but I'll have to take my chances.

Me: You never know until you try.

Ben: Isn't that the truth.

Me: It's getting late. I should probably go to bed.

Ben: Me, too.

Me: Goodnight, Benjamin. I'll see you tomorrow.

Ben: Goodnight, beautiful. You most certainly will.

NINE

BEN

I WASN'T sure if a weekend was long enough to bring Shannon around to the idea of dating. But by Monday morning —and especially after texting with her last night—my ability to hold back was at its breaking point. I still had another little surprise up my sleeve—and it was important that I give it to her. But I'd been a very patient man for a long time. Come what may, I was going to make my move. Today.

I drove down to Salishan early, so I'd be sure to see her before the day got away from both of us. But the first time I caught sight of her, she was in one of the utility vehicles with Cooper, about to head to the vineyards. Our eyes met and she smiled. I couldn't be sure from this distance, but she might have even blushed.

Yep. I was going for it. I just needed a chance to get her alone.

I still had work to do, so I filled my morning with tasks that needed doing. She and Cooper came back around noon, but he followed her into the Big House. A few minutes later, Leo called, asking if I could help him test the security system.

These boys really needed to get out of my way.

It was mid-afternoon before I made my way back to the Big House. I found Shannon in the main tasting room chatting with a few guests. Her hair was down today—she usually wore it back —and she was dressed in a dark blue shirt and beige pants.

Beautiful, as always.

Leaning one shoulder against the doorway, I met her eyes. Her face lit up with a smile and she held up a finger, asking me to wait.

Don't worry, Shannon. I've been waiting a long time for this. A few more minutes won't matter.

She finished talking to the guests and tucked her hair behind her ear as she walked over.

"Hi," she said, her voice soft.

With very few exceptions, I'd always stopped myself from touching her, no matter how strong the urge. Not today. I reached out and brushed her hair back behind her shoulder.

"Hi. You look beautiful today."

Her lips only twitched, but her smile lit up her eyes. "Thank you."

"Do you have a minute?"

She glanced over her shoulder. Brynn smiled at us from behind the bar.

"Sure," she said.

I loved this woman's kids as much as I loved her, but they were really cramping my style lately. I nodded to Brynn, then gently took Shannon's elbow.

She let me lead her into the hallway. Lindsey was at the front desk. That was no good. I heard noise coming from the kitchen. That wouldn't work. I didn't bother with the event room. People were always coming and going in there.

I pulled her down the hall and into the storeroom next to the kitchen.

"What are we—"

Instead of letting her finish her question—or answering it—I shut the door with my foot, pushed her up against the wall, and kissed her.

Finally. Oh my god, *finally*.

Bracing myself with one hand on the wall, I twined my fingers through her silky hair as her mouth softened against mine. I pressed my lips to hers, letting us both sink into the kiss. Felt her body relax.

With a soft exhale, she slid her hands around my waist, drawing me closer. I sucked on her lower lip, savoring my first taste of her. She was everything I'd imagined she'd be. Smooth and delicate. Delicious.

She parted her lips and I felt the tip of her tongue. A low growl rumbled in my throat as I delved into her mouth, letting my tongue slide against hers. She tilted her head and her hands moved up my chest. I craved her touch like a man starved. Her fingers found skin as she drew her hands around to the back of my neck.

All I could think was *more*. I needed more of her. More contact. More of her taste. I picked her up, pressing her back to the wall. Her legs hooked around my waist. Holding her ass in my hands, I kept kissing her. Deep and hungry. Long drags of my tongue against hers.

I'd meant to kiss her softly. Be a gentleman. But there was nothing gentlemanly about the way I was growling into her mouth. Squeezing her ass in my hands. There were decades of pent-up desire in this kiss, and I was done keeping it all inside.

I felt it in her, too. She kissed me back, just as passionately. Her arms wound tight around me, her fingers sliding through my hair.

Losing all sense of time, I kept kissing her. Reveled in this moment. I'd waited so damn long for this. Imagined it so many times. And the reality of kissing Shannon was better than anything I'd dare let myself dream.

This woman was everything.

In the back of my mind, I was aware of footsteps in the hallway outside. But I didn't care. The threat of interruption wasn't enough to make me stop. Not when I finally had her. When I could touch her and taste her lips. Kissing her was bliss.

Besides, I'd promised to kiss her breathless. And I was nothing if not a man of my word.

We made out in the storeroom for goodness knew how long. I wasn't exactly a young man anymore, but I was strong— holding her up was easy. And feeling her pressed against the wall with her legs around me was unbelievable.

Finally, I pulled away, just a little. Rested my forehead against hers. She was breathing hard, her arms still holding me tight. I let her legs down, slowly lowering her to the floor.

Her hands moved back to my chest and I kept my forehead to hers. Let us both catch our breath.

"You weren't kidding when you said you'd kiss me," she said, her voice soft.

I brushed her hair back from her face. "I always keep my promises."

"What happens now?"

That was a very good question. There was a part of me—a very insistent part—that wanted to drag her home right now and make love to her. But I knew she wasn't quite ready for that. Soon. But not yet.

"Will you have dinner with me?"

There was a hint of relief in her smile. "Yes, I'd love that."

"Are you free tonight?"

"I am."

"Can I pick you up at seven?"

She nodded. "Seven is good."

"Then it's a date."

Her eyes moved to my mouth and she slid one hand up to trace her fingers through my beard. I leaned in to kiss her again —gently this time.

"I suppose I have to let you get back to work," I said.

"Yeah, I suppose so. And I have to get ready. I have a date tonight."

"A date? He's a lucky man."

Her soft laugh was music to my ears. "I'm a lucky woman."

"It's about time, don't you think?"

"About time we get lucky?" she asked.

I groaned. "Dear god, Shannon, don't start talking like that. We're at work. You're going to get me in trouble."

She laughed again, then nibbled on her bottom lip while she touched my beard again. "I'll see you at seven."

"I'll be there."

She slipped out the storeroom door, glancing back at me over her shoulder before she left. I turned and leaned against the wall. Closed my eyes and let out a long breath.

God, that woman.

Tonight, I was going to give her the best date of her life.

TEN

SHANNON

IT WAS MID-AFTERNOON, but I didn't bother going back to work. I needed a little time to collect myself, so I went straight home.

The memory of Ben's kiss was still hot on my lips. He hadn't just kissed me. He'd consumed me. Never in my life had I been kissed like that. It had been thrilling and arousing. New and familiar all at once. It was Benjamin. My friend. The man who'd been a presence in my life for so long.

But this was a side of Ben I'd never known. A side of him I hadn't dared hope to experience.

And now, for the first time in a very long time, I had a date.

I decided to calm my nerves with a glass of wine and a hot bath. I soaked for a while, luxuriating in the water and the memory of Ben's beard against my skin. His lips on mine. It had felt better than I'd imagined.

And I realized how much I'd been missing that. The feeling of someone wanting me. Kissing and touching and connecting. I'd been missing intimacy for so long—since well before my marriage had ended. And the prospect of discovering it again was both exciting and a little scary.

After my bath, I dried off and slipped on my robe. I needed to decide what to wear tonight, so I stood in front of my closet, scrutinizing my choices.

I heard a knock downstairs, followed closely by someone calling my name.

"Shannon? You home?"

What was Zoe doing here?

"Upstairs," I called out.

I hoped she didn't need a babysitter. I was usually more than happy to watch Hudson, but tonight was another story.

"Oh good, you're getting ready," she said as she peeked through my partially-open door.

"What?"

Zoe came in, followed closely by Hannah and Amelia. Zoe had a garment bag hanging on her arm. Hannah had a small tote with a curling iron sticking out the top and Amelia carried an armful of makeup bags.

"What are you all doing here?" I asked.

"We're here to help you get ready for your date," Amelia said, her voice matter-of-fact.

"Help me... wait, how did you know I have a date?"

"Cooper saw you come out of the storeroom in the Big House and he said you looked all dreamy and weird and you walked right by him without saying anything," Amelia said. "And then a minute later he saw Ben come out of the storeroom, so he figured you two were in there together, which must mean, you know. So he asked Ben, and Ben said he was taking you out on a date tonight."

I shook my head. "If there's a downside to a family business, it's this."

Zoe lifted her eyebrows and set the garment bag on my bed. "Wow, Shannon. Getting freaky in the Big House? I'm impressed."

"We didn't *get freaky*," I said. "We just... kissed."

They all gasped at once.

"He kissed you?"

"It finally happened?"

"Go, Ben."

I held up my hands. "Okay, yes, he kissed me. And he asked me to dinner."

"This is so romantic," Hannah said. She swiped beneath her eyes and sniffed. "Sorry, I'm just a little emotional right now."

"And Ben asking you to dinner leads us full circle," Zoe said. "Let's get you date-ready."

"You're not going to try to get me to wax, are you?" I asked.

Zoe waved a hand. "No, it's too late for that. You need to give the skin a good twenty-four hours after waxing before someone gets in your lady bits."

"I'm going to dinner, Zoe. It doesn't have anything to do with my lady bits."

"Sure." Zoe's tone left little doubt that she really meant *yeah right*.

I shook my head. There was no point in arguing with her.

"You did shave your legs, though, right?" Amelia asked. "Just in case, I mean. It's always good to be prepared. Cooper's always saying that Ben taught him that, and I think it's a good lesson. And Ben burned his mattress already, so we all know what that means. Plus, smooth legs feel nice."

"Hold on," I said. "What did you say about Ben's mattress? He burned it?"

"Yeah, not that long ago," Amelia said. "I missed that one, which is such a bummer because the only time I got to go to a mattress burning was Leo's. And I don't know who else is going to do it, now. Maybe Grace will, I guess, but it seems like that might be stretching things, since she lives a little farther away.

Man, if I'd known that was going to be my one and only mattress burning, I would have taken some pictures."

Mattress burning was probably not a normal activity in most families. But this was the Miles family. My kids had burned mine first, after I'd kicked out my ex. Since then, it had become a symbol of casting off your old life, particularly when you were ready to move into a committed relationship.

But Ben had burned his mattress before we'd even been on a date? That meant two things, as far as I could tell. One, he wanted more than one date with me—perhaps more than just *dating*. And two, he was ready to welcome me into his bed.

A few days ago, that would have scared me. But everything was changing.

"You girls are so sweet to come over, but I'm fine," I said. "I'm sure I have something I can wear."

"Did you pick something already?" Hannah asked. "Can we see?"

I pulled a peach floral maxi dress out of my closet. "This is nice. And I've only worn it a few times."

"Nope," Zoe said.

"Why not?"

"Is he taking you to an Easter brunch?" she asked.

Amelia snickered and Hannah put her hand over her mouth.

"Come on, Shannon," Zoe said. "This is a *date*. With *Ben*. This is a big night and you deserve to look like the foxy mama you are."

"What do you suggest?" I asked, gesturing to my open closet.

"Keep an open mind." Zoe unzipped the garment bag, revealing black fabric inside. "I bought this a month or so ago, but I've never worn it. And I think it would look amazing on you."

She held up a sleeveless black dress. It had a V-neck that would dip far too low and a skirt that was far too short. It was gorgeous, but...

"I can't wear that," I said. "It's beautiful, but no. I couldn't."

"Just try it on," Zoe said, pushing it toward me.

"You really should," Amelia said. "It would be so pretty on you."

"I agree," Hannah said. "At least give it a try."

I took the dress from Zoe and held it out. It wasn't something I'd have picked for myself. But it did look like a date dress. And that's what this was. A date. So why not? I wasn't positive it would fit, but it wouldn't hurt to try it on.

I slipped the dress on and Zoe helped me zip it up in back. Running my hands down my hips, I smoothed it down, then turned so the girls could see.

"Holy shit, Shannon," Zoe said. "You're smoking hot in that thing."

"Yeah," Amelia said, her voice awed. "It's perfect."

Hannah sniffed and wiped her eyes. "I agree. Sorry, I don't know why I keep crying over everything lately."

"That would be pregnancy," Zoe said. "Shannon, I'm serious. You're stunning. Go look."

I moved to stand in front of my full-length mirror. I almost didn't recognize the woman looking back at me. My hair was still up in a bun from taking a bath, leaving my neck bare. The V-shaped neckline dipped down provocatively, and the fabric hugged my waist and hips. It was short, but not uncomfortably so, coming almost to my knees.

"Wow," I whispered.

"God, I can't wait for him to see you in this," Zoe said.

There was another knock on the door downstairs and all four of us gasped.

"He's not here yet, is he?" Amelia asked.

Hannah made for the bedroom door. "I'll stall him while you guys do makeup."

"Mom?" Brynn's voice called out from downstairs.

"Up here, Brynn," Zoe said.

I let out a breath as my daughter walked in.

She stopped in the doorway and set something down, her eyes widening. "Mom? Holy crap, look at you."

"She has a date with Ben," Amelia said.

Brynn's eyes grew even larger and she opened her mouth like she was going to say something. But nothing came out.

For a second, my heart sank. My kids all loved Ben, there was no question about that. But what if they didn't love the idea of me being with him?

"Brynn—"

"I'm so excited and happy and I almost don't know what to say so I guess I'm just going to wind up rambling like Amelia. This is so amazing, I can't even..." She paused and took a breath. "You really have a date with Ben? Are you serious? Tonight?"

"Yes."

She dashed into the room and threw her arms around me. I hugged her back, tears stinging my eyes.

"You're okay with it?" I asked.

"Are you kidding? I've been wishing you two would get together for... I don't even know how long. This is a dream come true."

"Thank you," I said softly.

"Oh my god, I can't," Hannah said. She took a sobbing breath and tears streamed down her face. "This is so beautiful and I love you all so much."

"Aw, Hannah," Zoe said. "Come here, sweetie."

Amelia widened her arms. "Group hug."

I found myself in the middle of my girls. My beautiful

daughter and the three amazing women who had joined our family. I loved these girls so much.

"Okay, we need to stop or we're never going to get Shannon ready," Zoe said. "Thank god you don't have makeup on yet."

I laughed and dabbed the corners of my eyes. "You girls are so wonderful. Thank you."

"I can't get over how bangin' you look in that dress," Brynn said. "Ben is going to lose his mind."

Running my hands over the dress, I smoothed it out again. "It's Zoe's."

"It's yours now," Zoe said.

"Oh, I almost forgot," Brynn said. She picked up the box she'd set in the doorway. "This was on your porch when I got here."

I took the box. It was small, wrapped in brown paper and tied with twine, like Ben's other gift had been. The tag was the same, a white card with my name written in his handwriting.

"I think it's from Benjamin," I said.

"We can go if you want to open it in private," Amelia said.

"That's okay." I set it down on the bed and pulled off the twine. I tore open the paper and lifted the lid. Inside was a small rectangular box.

"That looks like jewelry," Brynn whispered. I wasn't sure if she was talking to me or the other girls.

My heart felt fluttery again and my stomach did an excited little flip. I opened the box, revealing a silver necklace with a deep blue stone. I pulled it out and held it up. The stone sparkled, like it was filled with starlight.

The girls gasped and murmured *oohs* and *ahs* while I stared at the beautiful necklace.

"Wow," I breathed.

"Yeah, wow," Brynn said. "Put it on."

I handed it to Brynn and turned. She draped it around my

neck and fastened the clasp. The stone sat just below the dip in my throat, the blue gleaming against my skin.

"I can't believe he did this," I said. "After everything else, this too?"

"What else?" Brynn said.

"He sent me flowers," I said. "And did you see the lanterns hanging on the front porch? He made those out of old Salishan wine bottles. He sent them with a bottle of wine he'd saved from the first season he worked here. Then he sent a mug. It says *good morning, beautiful* on it."

"That's so sweet," Hannah said.

I nodded. "It was. And now this necklace."

"Wait," Amelia said. "Is that all? Flowers, then the wine bottles, then the mug, then the necklace? He didn't give you anything else recently?"

"That's it," I said. "Isn't that enough?"

"No, that's not what I mean," she said. "I just thought... never mind."

"Well, he did loan me a book, but that wasn't really a gift," I said. "It's from the library."

Amelia's eyes widened. "A *borrowed* book?"

"Yeah," I said. "He loans me books all the time."

"Don't you guys get it?" Amelia asked. She scrunched her shoulders. "I can't believe you don't see it. Oh my god, it's the cutest thing in the whole world. You really don't get it?"

"Get what?" Brynn asked.

"What Ben did with these gifts," Amelia said. "The flowers represent dating and courtship, right? But the rest. The wine bottles? They're something old. The mug? Something new. A library book is something borrowed. And the necklace?"

"Something blue," I said, touching the blue stone at my throat.

"Wow," Zoe said. "I knew Ben was good, but I had no idea he was *this* good."

"Oh my god," Brynn said. "Is he telling you he wants to marry you?"

I held the necklace between my fingertips and turned back to the mirror. They were right. Deep down, I knew. I'd felt it today when he'd kissed me. It hadn't simply been a few stolen minutes in a storeroom. Two people who'd been holding their attraction to each other in check for too long, finally finding the courage to unleash.

I'd tasted forever in that kiss.

"I think he is."

ELEVEN

SHANNON

THE GIRLS SCRAMBLED into the kitchen when we heard Ben's knock. They'd helped me with my hair and makeup, fussing over me like I was about to walk the red carpet, not have dinner with a man. I didn't even know where we were going. For all I knew, this dress and my black heels were overkill for what Ben had planned for us tonight.

But they'd done a good job. My hair was down, falling in soft waves around my shoulders. I hadn't worn this much makeup in a long time, but it was classy, not overpowering. I looked like I was ready for an evening out.

More importantly, I felt amazing.

I'd lost so much of myself over the years. In pouring everything I had into my family and our business, I hadn't saved much for me.

Ben had begun the process of uncovering the woman I was on the inside. Of helping me rediscover her. Tonight, my girls had helped me find a little more. Maybe it was just a little makeup and a dress. But really, it was so much more than that. It was the real me. A woman who'd been set aside for too long and who was desperate to be set free.

I walked to the door feeling more confident than I'd felt in years. I looked good, but more than that, I felt good. I felt beautiful. And no matter what else happened tonight, that was priceless to me.

Ben stood outside, looking unbelievably handsome in a dark sweater and slacks. His beard was neatly trimmed and he held a bouquet of flowers. He blinked at me, his mouth hanging open.

I smiled. "Hi."

"Oh, Shannon." His eyes flicked up and down. "You look incredible."

I smoothed my dress down, then touched the necklace at my throat. "Thank you. And thank you for this. It's beautiful."

"You're welcome."

"Am I overdressed?"

"No, you're perfect." He held out the flowers. "These don't hold a candle to how stunning you are."

Bringing them to my nose, I inhaled their scent. "They're beautiful. Thank you."

I hadn't noticed Brynn come out of the kitchen, but she was there, quietly taking the flowers.

"I'll put these in water," she whispered. "You go have fun."

"Thanks, Sprout," Ben said, winking at her. "Shall we?"

Always the gentleman, he helped me with my coat. My skin tingled as he pulled my hair from beneath the collar.

He offered me his arm and led me to his truck. Opened the passenger door for me and shut it once I was inside. He got in the driver's side and gazed at me for a long moment.

"Sorry, I can't seem to stop staring," he said.

"The girls helped me get ready."

"You look beautiful all the time, but this..." His eyes swept up and down again. "This is special."

"It's a special night."

"That it is," he said.

"Where are we going?"

He smiled. "I hope you don't mind, but I have something a little different planned for tonight."

"Oh?"

"Would you mind coming to my place?" he asked. "I made dinner."

I just about melted into a puddle on the floor. He cooked us dinner? "That sounds wonderful."

"Great."

The drive to his house was only a few minutes. He lived up the side of the mountain, with sweeping views of the town. And Salishan. He parked outside and went around to open the door for me. I felt his hand on the small of my back as we walked in.

In all the years Ben had lived here, I'd never been inside his house. Going in felt like crossing a line. One I wouldn't have dared cross before. But now? I was ready.

He shut the door behind us, then took my coat and hung it by the door.

Ben lived in a beautifully constructed log cabin. It was clean and cozy, with a leather couch in front of a wood-burning fire-place. His table was set for two, complete with candles, and the entire place smelled amazing.

"Dinner isn't fancy." He went into the kitchen and washed his hands. "Red wine-roasted chicken with herbs and some roasted vegetables."

"It smells delicious. Can I help?"

"No, I've got it." He uncovered the chicken and my mouth watered at the scent. "Unless you want to pour the wine."

"That I can definitely do."

I went to the table and poured us each a glass. A minute later he brought our food to the table, setting my plate in front of me.

"It's been a long time since someone cooked me dinner," I said.

He sat and met my eyes. "I know."

We started in on our meals—the food was delicious—and chatted about the usual things. My kids, Salishan, the last book he'd loaned me. Spending time with Ben had always felt easy and comfortable—so many things about this night were different, but that much hadn't changed. We talked and laughed as we ate, the mood relaxed, with a tantalizing buzz of anticipation humming in the background.

When we'd both finished our meals, Ben poured more wine. "Can I ask you a serious and rather personal question?"

"Of course."

"How are you?" he asked. "Be honest. And I don't mean how are you tonight."

I understood exactly what he meant. How was I after finding out about my ex-husband's lengthy infidelity. After an ugly and frustrating divorce. After the father of my children had almost cost me my home and been sent to prison.

"The truth?"

"Yes," he said, his voice emphatic.

"I'm getting better." I put my glass down and took a deep breath. "I put on a brave face for everyone, but when I found out that he had a mistress, I was devastated. I'd spent years staying strong for my kids. I was very good at it. But that almost broke me."

My eyes welled up with tears, so I paused. I didn't want to cry. Not here. Not now. Especially not over my bastard ex-husband. But these were feelings I'd never shared with anyone. It felt good to speak them aloud.

"So much of my life was a lie," I said, my voice quiet. "I didn't know the woman I'd become. How had I turned into a person who'd let a man walk all over her? I let things go and ignored the way he treated me, trying so hard to keep everything together. I did it for our kids, and for Salishan. Really, for everyone but me."

His eyes were full of sympathy and kindness as he looked at me. "I'm sorry, Shannon."

I took a deep breath. "I bent, but I didn't break. And now that it's all over, I can move on. I'm ready. So, to answer your question, I wasn't okay for a while. I was terribly hurt and alone. But so many good things have happened in the last couple of years, they drown out all the bad."

He reached across the table and took my hand, stroking the backs of my fingers. "I wish I could have done more to help. I understand what it's like to almost break."

I sensed something in his voice. A vulnerability—perhaps a willingness to share. I put my other hand over his. "Does it have something to do with why you came to Salishan all those years ago?"

"It does. I suppose my truth is that I was trying to disappear. I'd been going from place to place for a while by the time I landed here."

"Why were you trying to disappear?"

He took a deep breath. "Before I came here, I was married. My wife and I had a son. We'd named him Benjamin, after me. Called him Benny. When Benny was two, he and his mom were hit by a drunk driver. They were both killed instantly."

My eyes filled with tears. "Oh Benjamin, I had no idea. I'm so sorry."

He met my gaze. "It's okay. Really. Up until maybe ten years ago, I couldn't have choked that story out without needing a hell of a lot of whiskey. Took me a long time to heal after losing them."

"I can't even imagine."

"Sometimes, that thing you fear—the worst thing you can

imagine—actually happens. I lost everything that night, including a lot of who I was. I tried to drink away the pain for a while, but that didn't get me anywhere. So I left. Moved to a new town. I didn't feel any better there, so I left again. Kept doing that all the way across the country. Until I got here."

"What made you stay?"

He smiled. "Cooper."

"Really?"

"Not just Cooper. It was all of them. But Cooper started it. Do you remember the day we met?"

"I do. Cooper ran off and you found him in the vineyard."

He nodded. "You said you'd baked cookies and offered me one. Cooper gave me this look. It was so serious. Like he was telling me I better come to your house and have a cookie. So I did. I met your boys and those kids... they got to me. I'd been keeping people out, trying to stay numb. And they just waltzed in and took up residence right here." He tapped his chest above his heart.

"You stayed for them?"

"I didn't think of it that way at first," he said. "I thought just one more season, then I'd go. Another year would pass, and I'd tell myself maybe I'd stay one more. Meanwhile, your boys were growing, and I was teaching them things. Walking in the vineyards and showing them the plants and trees. Teaching them how to build fires and whittle sticks. Then Brynn came along, and I couldn't imagine not being around for them. Not seeing them grow up."

"I can't believe I never knew."

"Well, I never told anyone. And don't get me wrong, I didn't see your kids as replacements for my son. Nothing could ever replace him. But they saved me. They gave me a reason not to give up on life. A reason to plant some roots."

"They were your family," I said.

"They *are* my family."

"I don't know what we would have done without you," I said. "You were a dad to them in so many ways. Maybe you weren't trying to be. But you were the man they needed. You still are."

He cleared his throat. "Thank you. It's good to hear you say that."

"You were the man I needed, too."

"That was obviously more complicated," he said with a grin. "I won't pretend I didn't have feelings for you before I should have. I did. But I wasn't going to overstep."

I traced my finger over the rim of my wine glass. "I feel like I wasted so much time. You were right here, and I could have..."

"Don't think like that," he said. "Mostly because dwelling on your regrets is no way to live. Believe me, I know. I almost drowned in regret. But who knows, maybe it wouldn't have worked out before. I think we both needed to be ready."

"I think you're right."

"And the real question is..." He paused, meeting my eyes. "Can I be the man you need now?"

"That's not even a question."

The smile he gave me made my heart beat faster. Full of heat and suggestion. His eyes lingered on me like a soft caress. I didn't wilt under his gaze. A tingle of nervousness ran through my belly, but it felt good. Exciting.

Amelia had been right. I was glad I'd shaved my legs.

He broke eye contact and took my plate. "I should get this cleaned up."

"Can I help?"

"No. You're mine tonight..." He cleared his throat. "My guest tonight."

This man. He was awakening something in me—a piece of myself I'd lost. I felt her fire, smoldering inside, responding to

Ben's deep voice and soft touches. I wanted her back. And I wanted Ben to be the one to bring her out.

While he took our dishes to the kitchen, I got up and went to the window. Even in darkness, the view was beautiful. Lights in town winked and sparkled. Salishan's land spread out below us. You could see some of the winery from here, including my house.

How many times had Ben come to my house unannounced, bringing extra produce he claimed would go bad, or a book he thought I'd like? Had he been standing here, gazing down at my house? Knowing I was alone? My heart ached with gratitude.

And something else. A feeling, long denied, was blossoming inside me. It was more than thankfulness for the way Ben had quietly supported me. More than the friendship that had grown between us these last two years.

I loved him. I loved him down to my very soul. It was terrifying to admit. Loving Ben would mean being vulnerable—risking my heart again.

But I knew he was worth the risk.

I heard him approach. Felt his presence behind me as I stood in front of the window. A tingle ran down my spine as he moved closer.

He ran his hands down my arms and spoke in a low voice. "Thank you for having dinner with me."

"It was delicious."

His hands continued their slow caress, up and down my bare arms. He put his face in my hair and breathed in deeply. My eyes fluttered closed, my body relaxing at his touch.

He brushed my hair to the side and leaned in close, placing a kiss on the back of my neck. I let out a sigh, trembling at the feel of his lips on my skin.

Running his hands through my hair, he tilted my head to the side. He trailed hot kisses down my bared neck, each one harder than the last. Kissed across my shoulder while one hand held my hair and the other slipped around my waist, pulling me against him.

My breath came faster as he worked his way back up my neck. His body was warm and solid behind me, an anchor for my swiftly beating heart and legs that felt like liquid. His kisses grew harder, more aggressive. I felt his tongue lapping out against my skin. Soft scrapes of his teeth behind my ear.

"Shannon," he growled. "I have wanted you for so long."

A hot swirl of desire built inside me. I reached back and slid my fingers through his hair. "I've wanted you, too."

With his hands on my body and his mouth on my skin, all I could think was *finally*.

TWELVE

BEN

HOLDING SHANNON AGAINST ME, I kissed her neck. Took my time and savored her taste. I'd imagined this so many times. Hoped and wished for it. And now I had her. She was here, with me, melting in my arms.

I tightened my grip on her hair and pulled her head to the side. Kissed across her smooth skin. My other hand started to roam, sliding up her ribcage. She shuddered as I found her soft breast, squeezing it gently.

She looked so good tonight, in that sexy black dress. It had been all I could do not to stare at her all through dinner. Seeing her like this—dressed up for me—almost made me wish I'd taken her out. I wanted to show her off to the world. Walk with her on my arm, quietly boasting that this woman was mine.

There would be plenty of time for that. Tonight was about us—and only us. A chance for us to speak our truths and share our souls. There was more I had to say, but right now, all I could think about was the way her body felt against me. Her soft sighs as I kissed her neck and shoulder. As I touched her, feeling her curves.

She'd spoken the words aloud, and her body gave me the same answer. She wanted me, too.

I let her hair down and slid my hands around to the back of her dress. With my face in her hair so I could keep breathing in her scent, I slowly lowered the zipper. Slipped my hand beneath the fabric, caressing her waist, down the curve of her hip. Leaning in to nip at her earlobe, I tucked my fingers beneath the top of her panties and tugged them a little.

She gasped, her back arching, and I pressed myself against her. Let her feel what she did to me.

We were in front of the window, and although there was no one around to see in, I wanted her to be completely comfortable.

"Come here, beautiful." I encircled her wrist with my hand and gently turned her, leading her deeper into the room.

The fire crackled and the lights were low. With her facing me, I slid my hands into her hair and leaned in, kissing her delicate lips. She held my arms while our mouths tangled, as if she needed me to keep her upright.

I'd kissed her more thoroughly than I'd intended earlier today. And now, there was nothing holding me back. I kissed her deeply, passionately. Kissed her for every time I'd wanted to but couldn't. For every time I'd stared at her with longing in my heart, wishing we could be where we were now.

I pulled away and leaned my mouth next to her ear. "Would you like to come to my bedroom?"

"Yes."

That one word, spoken in that breathy voice, nearly undid me. My eyes rolled back and a low groan rumbled in my throat. I took her hand again and led her down the hall to my room.

A single lamp on the nightstand cast a soft glow. My room was furnished simply—dark wood, a comfortable bed, an upholstered chair by the window. I hadn't known if tonight would lead here, but I was prepared just the same. Clean sheets, closed curtains, and even a few candles ready to be lit if that was what she wanted.

Shannon stepped out of her shoes. I stood behind her and slipped her dress from her shoulders, slowly letting it drop to the floor. Leaned down to kiss her shoulder again. First one, then the other.

She turned to face me, nibbling her bottom lip. The shyness in her eyes made me want to scoop her into my arms. She met my gaze, then looked away.

Sensing her hesitance, I touched her chin and slowly lifted her face. "It's okay if you don't want to—"

"I do," she said quickly. She glanced down at herself. "It's just, I don't know how you're going to feel about the way I look."

I blinked at her a few times, honestly baffled. "The way you look? You're beautiful."

"But I'm far from perfect."

"Shannon, as far as I'm concerned, no one could be more perfect. Do you want to know why?"

She nodded.

"Because you're you. You're the most incredible, kind, smart, sexy woman I know. Your body is a work of art and I'm truly humbled that you'll share this with me."

"Why are you so wonderful?" she asked.

I shrugged. "I'm just Ben."

"Well, *just Ben*, you're still wearing all your clothes."

I didn't need any more encouragement than that. I pulled my sweater over my head and let it drop to the floor.

As we finished undressing, I watched her in awe. There was nothing but truth in what I'd said. She was flawed and human and utterly perfect.

Drawing her close, I slipped my arms around her. She ran her hands up my body, fingering my chest hair as I leaned down to kiss her. I ached for her, but didn't want to move too fast. I needed to relish every moment, every touch, every kiss.

I led her to the bed and pulled the covers down. We climbed in and I nudged her onto her back. Taking my time, I caressed her soft curves. Kissed her smooth skin.

She ran her hands over my arms and chest. My mouth found hers and I let my fingers trail to the apex of her thighs. She tipped her knees apart, and I slid my hand between her legs.

Moaning into my kiss, she tilted her hips. I caressed her, soft at first. Exploring, letting her relax into my touch. Rhythmic swipes of my thumb had her breathing hard, her cheeks flushed.

"So beautiful," I murmured, drinking in the moment. The woman I loved, lying here undressed and vulnerable.

Kissing and caressing, I lavished her body with affection until we were both frantic. Desperate for more. I climbed on top of her and settled between her legs, groaning at the feel of her skin against mine. So much heat and silky softness. She was everything I'd been wanting. Everything I'd craved for so long.

And now she was mine.

"Are you with me?" I asked.

"I'm with you."

I pushed inside her—slowly, carefully. She felt so good, it was hard to contain myself. She sighed, her eyes drifting closed, her hair fanned out across my pillow. I kissed her mouth, down to her neck, lost in the feel of her. In the way our bodies joined so perfectly, as if this had always been meant to be.

Then again, maybe it had.

Our movements began slowly—gentle and exploratory. But as we relaxed into each other, the heat between us rose. I thrust harder, feeling her body respond. Enjoyed the way she dug her fingers into my back.

We moved in sync, the tantalizing rhythm overtaking my

senses. I could feel her, taste her, smell her. Her gasps and moans spurred me on as I drew us both closer to climax. The feel of her was breathtaking. Aching pressure built, almost to the breaking point.

"That's it, beautiful," I growled into her ear as I thrust in hard. "You feel so good."

I felt the moment she let go, when she truly set herself free. She pressed her hands into my lower back, pulling me in deeper, and her hips rolled against me. Her head tilted back and her lips parted as she tightened around me.

"Benjamin, yes," she breathed.

I surrendered, giving her everything I had. Worshiped her, making love to her with reckless abandon. The tension in her body peaked as she started to come. I was only a heartbeat behind. My back stiffened and the pressure in my groin exploded. Burying my face in her neck, I groaned as I came in her, driving in hard until we were both spent.

Lifting up slightly, I found her lips with mine. She ran her fingers through my hair as I kissed her, a deep sense of contentment filling me.

"That was amazing," she whispered.

Smiling, I kissed her again. "Amazing doesn't even begin to describe it."

I rolled off and let her up so she could use the bathroom. As soon as she came back, I pulled her into bed with me and drew the covers over us. Wrapping my arms around her, I held her close. Kissed her forehead and breathed in her scent.

"Shannon?"

"Mm-hmm?"

I kissed her forehead again. "I love you."

A gentle shudder ran through her body and she took a shaky breath. "Oh, Benjamin. I love you too."

Tightening my arms around her, I squeezed my eyes shut.

In the space of an evening, my dreams had all come true. After years of longing, I could finally love her.

"I want you to know that I'll give you whatever you need," I said. "If you need to go slow, we can take our time. But now that I have you, I don't intend to let you go. Ever."

"I'm not letting you go either," she said. "I need you, Benjamin. And I need to belong to you. I can't risk my heart for anything less."

I nudged her onto her back and gently caressed her cheek. "Beautiful, I'm yours forever. Like I said, I'll give you what you need, but I'd marry you first thing in the morning if I could."

She laughed. "Is that what the gifts meant? Something old, something new, something borrowed, something blue?"

"That is exactly what they meant." I kissed her again. "We've both waited a long time for this. I don't want to go a second without you."

Her smile had a hint of mischief. "Benjamin, are you proposing to me on our first date?"

"I'm simply suggesting that we can skip over *dating*. I don't need more time. I know exactly what I want. To spend the rest of my life loving you."

"I don't need time either," she said.

I hadn't exactly planned for this moment to happen now, but like I'd taught the boys, it was important to always be prepared. I grinned at her and reached over to my nightstand. Pulled a small square box out of the drawer.

"Oh my god," Shannon said. "You have a..."

"Like I said, I know what I want. I want you to be mine, always." I opened the box, revealing a vintage-style halo diamond ring. "Shannon, my love, will you marry me?"

She met my eyes and reached up to touch my face. "Yes, Benjamin. I would love to marry you."

I kissed her, although I couldn't stop smiling. "If you were ever wondering what it looks like when all a man's dreams come true, it looks like this."

She touched my face again, running her fingers through my beard. "Thank you for waiting for me."

"My darling Shannon, you are more than worth the wait."

EPILOGUE

BEN

I'D BEEN to a lot of weddings here at Salishan. Helped set up and decorate for hundreds of them. Attended quite a few. A handful of friends had wed here over the years. Then Roland and Zoe celebrated their second—and forever—nuptials. I had the honor of walking Brynn down the aisle when she married Chase. Last month, Leo had married Hannah in the back garden. And although they weren't married just yet, I had a feeling Cooper and Amelia would do so here, when it was their time.

But today? On a beautiful summer evening in June, it was my turn.

Standing in front of a mirror in the groom's dressing room, I adjusted my suit jacket. Ran a hand over my beard. I wasn't the least bit nervous for the ceremony that would bind me to Shannon for the rest of my life. This was our day. The moment I'd been waiting for. I couldn't wait for her to officially become my wife. For us to become a family.

Although really, we already were.

We'd spent the last few months since that first night together—that first date that had been so much more—enjoying our newfound freedom to be a couple. She'd asked me to move in right away, which suited me just fine. I didn't want to spend a single night without her. I'd moved into her house, and our lives had melded together effortlessly.

Her kids had been ecstatic to learn we planned to get married. They seemed to see things the way we did. We knew what we wanted for our lives—being together forever wasn't a question—so why waste more time?

Shannon and I loved each other. Our bond had been forged in friendship, the fire of our affection kindled long ago. Now, we both had exactly what we wanted. Each other.

We also had Salishan—thriving now, thanks to Roland's expert care—a group of adult children and significant others we both loved and had the pleasure of seeing regularly, a grandson about to turn one, and a granddaughter on the way.

I'd lost a family once, and it had nearly destroyed me. But the family I was gaining filled my heart and soul. I loved these people. Had for years. They were my life.

And what a life it was.

"Ben." Cooper poked his head in through the door. "Holy shit, you look awesome. You're very *James Bond*, do you know that? And let's be honest, no one would be surprised to find out you're a secret agent."

"Thanks, Cooper."

He leaned his head back into the hallway. "Chase, get your ass over here. If Zoe catches you trying to sneak food again, she'll punch us both."

"I wasn't sneaking food," Chase said as he came into the room. Cooper followed. They were both dressed in dark suits and ties.

"I swear to god, Chase, I can't take you anywhere," Cooper said.

Chase just laughed and licked something off his fingers.

Roland came in, followed closely by Leo. Roland's tie was straight, his suit perfect. Leo's thick beard was trimmed and he had his hair pulled back. His tie hung around his neck and his shirt collar was unbuttoned.

"How am I ready before you?" Cooper asked Leo. "You're supposed to be the quiet responsible one."

"I thought Roland was the responsible one," Chase said.

"You obviously don't remember Roland in high school," Leo said, lifting his chin to button his collar.

"Well, I'm definitely not the responsible one, but I'm rocking this suit today," Cooper said. "And you guys all look fucking great. Here, let me."

Leo only flinched a little as Cooper helped him with his tie. It was such a relief to have Leo back. He'd always have some quirks, and the things he'd been through had left their mark. But he was happier, and healthier, than I'd seen him in years. That ring on his finger certainly had a lot to do with it.

I was proud of Leo. Proud of all these boys. They'd grown into good men. They understood what it meant to be men of their word, to take responsibility, and use their strength to protect the ones they loved. I liked to think I had a part in that, however small. Seeing them all find love, and be admirable men to the women in their lives, made me feel like I'd accomplished something good in the years I'd spent here.

"Who has a bottle of something?" Cooper asked. "This is a big day. We need to toast."

Chase headed for the door. "I'll be right back."

"Don't get in trouble with Zoe," Cooper called after him. "I'm supposed to be watching you."

"*You're* supposed to be watching *him*?" Roland asked.

"There's bacon-wrapped stuff in the kitchen," Cooper said. "You know that guy can't be trusted around anything wrapped in bacon."

"Neither can you," Roland said.

"True."

"I'll make sure he doesn't eat all Mom's hors d'oeuvres," Leo said with a grin, and followed him out the door.

Chase and Leo came back a minute later with five glasses and a bottle of Salishan cabernet. I poured and we all raised our glasses.

"To Ben," Cooper said. "The man who taught us most of what's worth knowing in this life."

"Who gave us an example of what a man should be," Roland said.

"Whose smooth badassery continues to be an inspiration," Chase said.

"And who never gave up on any of us," Leo said. "Including Mom."

"Welcome to the family," Cooper said. "Officially."

We clinked our glasses and I was glad they didn't keep talking. I took a sip to cover the swell of emotion that bubbled up my throat. Their acceptance meant the world to me. It wasn't that I'd doubted it. But hearing them say it out loud made my chest ache a bit.

Jamie knocked on the door and poked her head in. "The ladies are waiting. Are you ready?"

I glanced in the mirror one last time. "Absolutely."

Our wedding was a small affair. Just our family, a few friends, and the other Salishan employees. We'd set it up like the old harvest parties we'd thrown, years ago. Strings of twinkle lights sparkled in the garden and there were tables with food and wine spread out on one side. Our guests sat at the smaller tables, or stood with wine glasses in their hands.

Shannon hadn't wanted all the pomp and circumstance of a full ceremony. We had a minister here to do the honors beneath a trellis draped with flowers and lights.

She stood near the trellis, dressed in an ivory lace gown. Her hair was curled, and the soft lights made her skin glow.

I stopped and watched Brynn place a circlet of flowers on her head. My Shannon. So beautiful. Maybe it was a cliché to say so, but she took my breath away. Especially today.

She glanced over and our eyes met. Her smile lit up her whole face. If I had one goal left in this life, it was to see her smile like that as often as possible. Making her happy was my greatest joy.

I crossed the distance to her and took her hands in mine. "Are you ready for this?"

"Absolutely," she said.

I met Roland's eyes and nodded. He and the other boys passed the word for everyone to take their seats while the minister came to the front with us.

Shannon and I stood, hands clasped, facing each other while the minister began. There wasn't much to our little ceremony. A few words, then it was time for us to say our vows.

"Benjamin," she began. "Today I have the privilege of marrying my best friend. The man who has been there for me for better or worse, in sickness and in health, through good times and bad, all long before we said a single vow. And come what may, I promise to honor this union and love you with my whole heart for the rest of my life."

Then it was my turn. My words were simple, but they were my truth. And I was a man of my word. "Shannon, my love for you is endless. I promise to be yours, always. I will be faithful in word and deed and I will love you and care for you until I take my last breath."

Tears shone in her eyes as she smiled up at me.

Roland and Zoe stepped up and handed us the rings. The minister nodded.

I took Shannon's hand and slipped the ring on her finger.

"With this ring, as a token of my love and fidelity, I thee wed."

She lifted my hand and placed the ring on my finger, repeating the same phrase. "With this ring, as a token of my love and fidelity, I thee wed."

"By the power vested in me, I now pronounce you man and wife." The minister smiled. "You may now kiss the bride."

Grinning, I brushed her hair back from her face. Leaned in close and placed my lips against hers. I kissed her softly at first. Then I slid my arms around her, drew her against me, and kissed her harder.

She threw her arms around my neck as our guests clapped and cheered. I picked her up off her feet and twirled her around. I was just so damn happy, I couldn't help myself.

I set her down and the kids all mobbed us. Cooper almost knocked me over, and he picked his mom up and spun her around too. I got big hugs from all the girls—Amelia, Zoe, and Brynn got to me first. Then Hannah, Grace, and Naomi. Elijah, looking adorable in his little suit, gave me a big high five. Chase hugged me tight, as did Roland. Even Leo, which meant a lot to me. I knew how he felt about being touched.

There were more hugs and congratulations from the rest of our guests. Then more food was brought out, wine served, and the celebration began.

I stood with my arm around Shannon and watched it all unfold. It was like seeing the last piece of a puzzle finally click into place. Everything was as it should be. I was married to the woman I'd loved for so long. My kids—I could really call them mine, now—were all happy. We had the joy of grandchildren. A home we both loved.

I had everything a man could want—certainly everything I'd ever wanted. Love. Family. Comfort. This was my life. They were my life. After everything we'd been through, we had each other. We had this. And that meant we had it all.

BONUS EPILOGUE

GRACE

TWO YEARS later

I STOOD OUTSIDE THE HOUSE, a set of keys dangling from my fingers. *My* keys. A jolt of excitement sent a little shiver down my spine. I'd done it. I'd planned and saved for years for this. And today, after signing paperwork until my hand felt like it was going to fall off, the house was mine.

A tangle of blackberry bushes covered the front window—most of the windows, actually. The front yard was knee-high grass and weeds, the fence was rotting, and that was just the outside. The interior was going to be a total gut job. At least the structure was sound. It needed a lot of drywall repair, but the walls were sturdy, and the roof was good.

The rest? It was pretty much a disaster. It needed a new kitchen, new bathrooms, new flooring, new paint, new windows. My realtor had tried to talk me out of buying it. As had my mom.

But this was more than just a house. It was a dream. A dream I was fighting to keep alive.

Asher and I had walked by this house on the way home from school every day for years. Most kids crossed to the other side of the street, calling it haunted or creepy. Not me and Asher. We'd both loved the old abandoned house on Evergreen Street. Years ago, we'd made a pact that we'd buy this house, together. It was where we were going to live our life. Start our family.

The plan had been to buy it after we were married. But those plans had been interrupted. Asher wasn't here. He was in prison.

Another shiver ran down my spine, but this one wasn't excitement. It was cold fear. It ran through my veins whenever I thought about Asher and what he was going through.

I took a deep breath. Smelled the fresh air and shook off my dark thoughts. There wasn't anything I could do about Asher right now. He wouldn't be gone forever. And when he got out, he'd come back to a dream that I'd turned into reality. Our dream. This house.

A strange way to cope with your fiancé being in prison? Probably. But I wasn't going to sit around doing nothing for eight years while I waited for him to come home.

My phone rang and I pulled it out of my pocket. It was Shannon, my father's ex-wife. My mother had unknowingly been the other woman in an affair, having two children with Lawrence Miles—me and my much younger brother, Elijah. Four years ago, I'd gone looking for my father—he'd gone deadbeat dad on my little brother—and discovered he was not only married, but had four other children.

It had been a shock to everyone, but my new family had embraced me and Elijah—and my mom. Mom had become good friends with Shannon. We'd been at Shannon's wedding two years ago when she'd married Ben Gaines. And when my mom had married Jack Cordero last year, Shannon had been her matron of honor.

I swiped to answer her call. "Hey, Shannon. Aren't you still in Barbados?"

"We are," Shannon said. "But I wanted to call and see if the house closed today."

"It sure did." I walked up to the front door. "I'm here now. I just got the keys."

"Congratulations. Benjamin says congratulations, too."

"Thanks. It's so sweet of you to call."

"Of course," she said. "Send me some pictures if you get the chance. We're here another week, but when we get back, I want to come see it in person."

"Definitely," I said. "Are you guys having fun?"

"This place is paradise," she said, her voice a little dreamy. "We're having a great time."

"I love that. You guys go get a yummy tropical drink or something. Enjoy yourselves. You certainly deserve it."

"Thanks, Grace," she said. "We'll see you next week."

"Bye."

I ended the call and slipped my phone in my back pocket. It was the moment of truth.

The key stuck in the lock. I had to jiggle it to get the doorknob to turn. That was fine, I'd change the locks anyway. That was the first thing Jack had said—*make sure you change the locks, Grace*. I liked my new stepdad. Navigating the new relationship had been a little tricky for me, but he sure did love my mom.

After jiggling the key a little more, I finally got the door open.

The interior was just as dilapidated as I remembered. But all I could see was potential. New paint, new floors, cozy furniture. I was going to take this old abandoned house and turn it into a home.

Before I'd even shut the door, a truck pulled up on the street. I'd invited my siblings to come see the house. My brother Cooper hopped out and pointed through the windshield at his wife, Amelia. It looked like he was telling her to wait. He went around to the passenger side and helped her out, keeping a firm grip on her arm, as if he was afraid she'd fall without him.

Of course, Amelia was a little off-balance. As tall as she was, I was surprised her pregnancy was showing so soon, but she had the cutest baby belly. It hadn't been long after their wedding that they'd announced Amelia was pregnant. I wondered if they knew if the baby was a boy or a girl yet. So far, they hadn't said.

Cooper stopped, his eyes widening as he took in the house. "Holy shit, Gracie, what the hell did you buy? This place is falling apart."

"I told you it was a fixer-upper. Hey, Amelia."

"Hey. The house is..." Amelia glanced around. "I bet it's going to be nice someday, but I kind of agree with Cooper."

I waved a hand. "I know. It's a lot of work, but it'll be fine. The inside is... well, it's not much better, but do you want to see it anyway?"

"Yes," Amelia said brightly. She looked adorable in a light blue t-shirt that said *Beauty and the Bump.*

Cooper had traded his cute husband t-shirts—which had replaced his extensive collection of boyfriend t-shirts—for new dad shirts. The last time I'd seen him, his shirt had said *future awesome daddy.* This one said *Sorry Ladies, This DILF is Taken.*

"Come on in." I moved aside and held the door open.

"You're right, the inside isn't better," Cooper said. He kept a firm grip on Amelia's arm as they stepped over a pile of debris. "Careful, baby."

"Yeah, but it's going to be so beautiful when it's done." I heard another car pull up outside. "I'll see who's here, but you guys are free to look around."

Cooper eyed the place warily, as if dangers to his pregnant wife lurked everywhere.

I went outside and waited on the front step while Leo and Hannah unloaded their little family. Their daughter Madeline was about twenty months, and their newest addition, a son named Zachary, had been born five months ago. Madeline had been a surprise, but they'd loved being parents so much, they hadn't waited long to have another baby.

Leo's hair was shorter than it used to be, but he still had a thick beard. He held Zachary up against his shoulder. Madeline slipped one hand in his, the other in her mom's, as they walked up the path.

"I know," I said, holding up a hand. I could see the doubt on their faces. "It needs a lot of work."

"No, it has so much potential," Hannah said. "I love it."

Motherhood looked great on Hannah. Despite the splotch on her shirt that was probably baby spit-up, she looked fantastic. She and Leo had moved into the house they'd built on Salishan property shortly before Zachary had been born.

"You have such a great eye for color, I'm totally going to pick your brain," I said.

"I'd love to help," Hannah said.

"Uncle Cooper?" Madeline asked, looking up at her dad.

"Yeah, sweetheart, I think Uncle Cooper and Auntie Amelia are already here."

"They're inside," I said. "I don't know if there's anything sharp on the floor, so we'll need to be careful with her."

"I've got her," Hannah said, scooping Madeline up and perching her on her hip. "Should we go see Auntie Grace's new house?"

"Yeah," Madeline said, her little pigtails bobbing as she nodded.

"Go on in," I said. "Cooper and Amelia are in there somewhere."

"We can wait until everyone gets here for the official tour," Leo said.

"Sure," I said. As if on cue, two more cars pulled up. "And here they are."

Brynn and Chase got out with their dog, Scout. Brynn held his leash to keep him from running off.

"Scout, chill," Brynn said. "He loves car rides, but I think he loves getting out in a new place even more."

"Scout, sit," Chase said, his voice authoritative. Scout immediately obeyed and Chase scratched his head. "Good boy."

"Hey, you guys," I said. "Thanks for coming. You can bring Scout inside, but be careful. I don't know what he'll find in there."

"We'll keep an eye on him," Brynn said.

Roland and Zoe had pulled up behind Brynn and Chase. Roland got their three-year-old son, Hudson, out of the car. Zoe was pregnant with their second child, a girl this time.

"Hey, Zoe," I said. "How are you feeling?"

She leaned against the car, resting her hand on her belly. "Not bad, all things considered. Four weeks and we get to meet her."

"How does Hudson feel about having a baby sister?" I asked.

Zoe shrugged. "He says he's excited. But I think he figures this baby will be like his cousin Zachary. He'll come over and then leave when he gets fussy. We'll see how he feels about her when she's in his house all the time and he has to share his parents with her."

Roland came around, holding Hudson's hand. "Huddy, can you say hi?"

"Hi, Auntie Grace," he said.

"Hi, buddy," I said. "Listen, I told Leo and Hannah this too, but I don't know what you'll find on the floors in there, so just be careful. It's... well, it's a mess."

"No problem." Roland picked up Hudson. "Come on, buddy, let's go check out the new house."

I followed everyone inside, then showed them around. They meandered through the house, peeking in bedrooms and wandering through the kitchen and living rooms. It wasn't very big, but the lot had room to add on if we wanted to, down the road. Of course, making it livable was the first step, and it was going to be a while before that happened.

It was fun to see everyone with their growing families. My family dynamic had changed so much in the last several years. First with discovering four new siblings, then with my mom getting married. They were good changes, but it had taken some time to process.

And it was sad not having Asher here to share in it. We should have been married by now. Maybe even starting our own family. I wrote him letters regularly, so of course I'd told him everything. But when he got home, these people would be strangers to him. Moments like this made my chest ache with the pain of missing him.

"Oh, hey, we're all here," Cooper said, as if just realizing that fact. Glancing at Amelia, he grinned. "Should we tell them?"

"Tell us what?" Brynn asked. "Oh my god, did you find out if the baby is a boy or a girl?"

Amelia's face lit up with a grin to match her husband's. "We did."

The room went quiet, as if everyone was holding their breath. I certainly was.

"Okay, first of all, I knew this from the beginning," Cooper said. "I can even tell you where we conceived, that's how soon I knew she was preggers. We were—"

"Stop," Hannah and Zoe said together.

"Coop, know your audience, buddy," Zoe said, gesturing to the two very curious children looking at him with wide eyes.

"Oh, right," Cooper said. "I'm going to have to get used to that, aren't I? Anyway, I'm just saying I totally called it. Didn't I, Cookie?"

"That's actually true," Amelia said. "I didn't even know I was pregnant, and Cooper looked at me one morning and said I looked pregnant, and he wanted the record to show that he thought it was twin boys. And I said that was probably impossible, but you never know. And we found out yesterday he was right."

The room went dead silent. Even among the dust and debris, you could have heard a pin drop.

"Did you just say twins?" Brynn asked.

Amelia beamed. "Yep. Both boys."

"Holy shit," Leo said. "Two baby Coopers?"

Cooper puffed out his chest and put a protective hand over Amelia's belly. "Is anyone really surprised? Of course I'd make two babies at once."

"This is amazing," Brynn said, rushing over to hug Amelia.

"Aw, you big goofball," Zoe said, hugging Cooper.

"Congrats, you guys," Roland said. "Wow, life is definitely getting interesting."

"Okay, Chase and Brynn," Zoe said. "When is it your turn?"

Brynn and Chase smiled at each other. "We're talking about it," Brynn said. "Soon."

"Do Mom and Ben know it's twins yet?" Roland asked.

"Nah, we'll tell them when they get back," Cooper said.

Madeline tugged on Leo's pant leg. "Daddy, are Grandma and Grandpa coming?"

"No, sweetheart," Leo said. "They're still on vacation. But they'll be back soon."

I glanced around at our broken-down surroundings. This was sweet, but we didn't need to keep standing around in my dilapidated house. "Well, now that you've seen it, we can go get some food or something. It'll be a while before I'm ready to entertain guests. But there are a bunch of good restaurants in town."

"Okay, but can we talk about how scary this house is?" Cooper asked. "Seriously, Gracie, this place looks like it's going to cave in."

Everyone looked around, murmuring in agreement.

"You know, we can help," Chase said.

"Thank you," I said. "I appreciate that, but I didn't ask you guys to come over here to put you to work."

"Yeah, but—"

Chase was interrupted by the sound of a loud engine outside. A very loud engine, followed by rowdy voices. I sighed. Of course they were here.

"Hang on a second," I said, and went to the front door.

Four men poured in, still talking to each other. Arguing, really. Typical brothers.

"Guys," I said, raising my voice so they'd hear me.

They all stopped, looking around—whether at the house or my family, I wasn't sure.

"So, guys, these are my brothers and sisters and their families. Roland, Zoe, and their son Hudson. Chase and Brynn, and the furry one is Scout. That's Leo and Hannah, and their little ones are Madeline and Zachary. And that's Cooper and Amelia." I paused to take a breath and gestured to the newcomers. "These guys are my fiancé's brothers. Evan, Levi, Logan, and Gavin Bailey."

"We've met," Logan said, and pointed at Brynn. "I was part of the entertainment at her bachelorette party."

"Oh right, the firefighter," Brynn said.

"Dude," Cooper said, pointing at Levi and Logan. "Are you grown-up twins? We're having twins. It's like seeing into the future."

"Identical," Logan said, glancing at his brother. "Sweet, man. Are yours boys?"

"Yep."

Logan grinned. "Awesome."

"Grace, can we talk about this?" Levi asked, looking around, his brow furrowed. "This place is worse on the inside."

"Exactly," Cooper said. "I like him."

"I know, I know." I put my hands up. "It's a fixer-upper. That means it needs a lot of fixing. But I got a full inspection, so I know what I'm dealing with."

"Can I get a copy of that?" Levi asked, wandering farther inside.

"Later," I said.

Logan put his hands on his hips. "I don't think it's that bad. Don't worry, Grace. We'll whip this place into shape."

My brothers glanced at each other, giving subtle nods, as if acknowledging that I'd be fine. And that was true. Asher's brothers had always taken care of me. His whole family had.

"Who wants pizza?" I asked.

Hudson's hand shot into the air. "Me."

Madeline glanced at her cousin and giggled, then copied him. "Me."

"All right, Baileys, scoot," I said, trying to shoo Asher's brothers out the door. "You can come with us to pizza, but I don't think any of us wants to hang out here in all the dust anymore."

"That's fine, Grace," Evan said. He was the second oldest, and also tallest, at six-foot-four. "We're on our way to Gram's anyway."

"But, pizza," Gavin said. He was the baby of the family.

"Later, Gav," Logan said, slipping on a pair of sunglasses. "Grace, we'll see you later. Miles fam, nice to see you."

The Baileys said goodbye, then went out and piled into Logan's muscle car. It ran some of the time, so he loved driving it when it did. The engine started with a loud rumble as the rest of us made our way outside.

I gave everyone the name of the pizza place and basic directions. My hometown wasn't very big, so I didn't think they'd have any trouble finding it. They all got in their cars while I locked up.

I had to jiggle the key again to get it to lock. With a deep breath, I touched my fingertips to the door. One step closer. The house we'd dreamed of was mine, and when Asher got home, it would be ours. I'd waited six years. Only two left.

I'd survived this long without him. I could wait a little longer.

AFTERWORD

Dear Reader,

It's with so many feelings that I write this final chapter in the Miles family series.

So. Many. Feelings.

This novella exists because of you. When I mapped out the series, I'd known Ben and Shannon were going to get their happily ever after. But I hadn't planned feature them in their own story. In my original series outline, Ben and Shannon's story unfolded across the four series novels, culminating with their HEA in Leo's book.

But you, my lovely readers, picked up on Ben's unrequited love for Shannon in the very first book. And so many of you asked for their story, I decided to write it.

I realize this is short—it is a novella, after all—and I know the end will be met with cries of, "More!" But this was the part of their story left to be told. We get to see them slowly coming together across the series. They gradually allow themselves to feel what they feel for each other. Their friendship blossoms.

We see hints that they spend time together. That Ben is the quiet support Shannon so desperately needs.

The part of their story left to tell was the final push. I wanted to show Ben deciding it was time to openly pursue the woman he'd loved for so long. And allow Shannon to come to terms with the fact that her life wasn't over. That she could still have love—real love—even after everything she'd been through.

I ran into an unexpected challenge while writing this book. Although I didn't see Shannon as MY mom, she had been THE mom throughout the series. How was I going to write her as a heroine? And what were readers going to think of the steamy parts?

My solution was to sink into both of them as characters. In the beginning, Shannon is focusing on her family and Salishan. She's not thinking of herself as a woman who might date, or love, or experience intimacy. But as Ben showers her with attention, making his intentions clear, she begins to see herself in a new way. She rediscovers a part of herself she'd thought was gone—the part that craves physical connection and intimacy. My hope was that you would discover that side of Shannon right along-side her. That by the time she and Ben sleep together, you're as ready for it as she is.

And Ben. That sweet, swoony, patient man. I always knew it was his love of the Miles kids that first prompted him to stay at Salishan. His love for Shannon blossomed later, and it was not an easy thing for him to live with. But his dedication and loyalty to that family ran deep. He loved them as his own, and he was willing to stay because of it. They were his family.

And now it's official.

It's so hard to say goodbye to this crazy, wonderful family. I had no idea when I began this journey—thinking about a family that owns a winery, wondering who they were and what their stories would be—that they would lodge themselves so deeply in my heart. I've spent countless hours with them. I've dreamt of them. And I've done my absolute best to make their stories heartwarming and wonderful.

Thank you for loving them with me. Thank you for reading their stories and laughing and crying and swooning. I hope that this series has brought you a little bit of happiness. Maybe touched your heart just a bit.

Family series are so my jam, so this certainly won't be the last. In fact, it won't be the last time you see these characters. Grace Miles, their half-sister, is going to be the first heroine in my next family series, the Bailey Brothers. So I'm sure we'll get glimpses of the Miles family again as they all live out their happily ever afters.

Thank you so much for reading.

CK

ACKNOWLEDGMENTS

Thank you, first and foremost, to my readers for loving these characters, and this family. This novella is for you.

Thank you to the team of people who work so hard to make these books possible. Elayne Morgan for her fantastic editing. Cassy Roop for a beautiful cover. My beta readers, Nikki and Jodi, for taking time out of their schedules to provide feedback.

Thank you to my family, as always. Without your loving support, I'd never be able to do what I do. Thanks for putting up with my weird job.

ALSO BY CLAIRE KINGSLEY

His Heart

A poignant and emotionally intense story about grief, loss, and the transcendent power of love.

Book Boyfriends

Hot romcoms that will make you laugh and make you swoon.

Book Boyfriend

Cocky Roommate

Hot Single Dad

The Always Series

Smoking hot, dirty talking bad boys with some angsty intensity.

Always Have

Always Will

Always Ever After

The Jetty Beach Romance Series

Sexy small-town romance series with swoony heroes, romantic HEAs, and lots of big feels.

Behind His Eyes

One Crazy Week

Messy Perfect Love

Operation Get Her Back

Weekend Fling

Good Girl Next Door

The Path to You

The Jetty Beach Box Set Books 1-4

ABOUT THE AUTHOR

Claire Kingsley writes smart, sexy romances with sassy heroines, swoony heroes who love their women hard, panty-melting sexytimes, romantic happily ever afters, and all the big feels.

She can't imagine life without coffee, her Kindle, and the sexy heroes who inhabit her imagination. She's living out her own happily ever after in the Pacific Northwest with her husband and three kids.

www.clairekingsleybooks.com

Made in the USA
San Bernardino,
CA

59019002R00085